The Era of the Orb

By Colin Dunbar

Keep up to date: Follow @colinbdunbar on Instagram!

Content Warning: substance use/abuse, violence

Copyright © 2021 Colin Dunbar

ISBN 9798630747235

All rights reserved. No part of this publication may be reproduced, distributed, or transmitted in any form or by any means, including photocopying recording, or other electronic or mechanical methods, without the prior permission of the publisher, except in the case of brief quotations in critical reviews and certain other non-commercial uses permitted by copyright law.

This is a work of fiction. Names, characters, places, and incidents either are the product of the author's imagination or are used fictitiously. Any resemblance to actual persons, living or dead, events, or locales is entirely coincidental.

For any inquiries, please contact me by email at colin@thedunbars.ca

Table of Contents

Judgement	**7**
Redemption	8
Solitary Confinement	**21**
The Walls Have Eyes	22
The Curse of a Past Life	**59**
Wealth of Blood	62
An Omen	**82**
Liquorice the Cat	89
The Warden	**95**
Personal Space	106
A Bag of Chips	**112**
The Perfect Family	117
The Confrontation	**134**
Channel Four News	145
Static Interference	**148**

I Want to Be a Good Person 159

Identity 182

I Need to Be a Good Person 194

Acknowledgements 200

About the Author 200

Also by Colin Dunbar 201

Judgement

I ran.

I could barely hear the

blaring alarm over the sound of the

other prisoners cheering me on. Some were

applauding me; others were looking for a place to

hide. Then, there was a new sound. The fast stomping

of a guard's combat boots. One caught up to me and tried

to grab me by the collar. I threw my elbow back, felt it hit

something, and the tension in my collar loosened as the

guard lost their grip. I continued to run and made a sharp

turn around the corner of the prison hall, bursting through

an exit door. Guards surrounded the perimeter. This was

the closest I had ever made it to getting out. Bullets

started to soar through the air around me, and

I felt a sudden sharp pain in the back of my

head. With a thud, I collapsed

to the ground. Yet another

life wasted.

Redemption

Three men in suits sat at a long conference table with a briefcase resting in the middle.

They didn't know I was there, hiding in the back of one of their minds, waiting for my moment.

"Alright, I'll give you fifty each. I keep it, and neither of you mentions this again," Isaac said.

"Fifty ain't shit. I could hire a hit on both of you, take the case, and still have fifty leftover after selling it back to Loch," Abraham replied.

"Two hundred, then?" Isaac asked.

"You think the case is worth two hundred thousand?" Jacob said.

"We're talking millions here, Jacob. Let the adults discuss," Abraham said, "and Isaac, I think your offer is an insult. I'll give five hundred and, obviously, you two need to stay silent."

Jacob just needed a little nudge along, so I took control for a moment.

"Six-hundred," Jacob declared.

"Oh? Someone thinks they can outbid me now, do they?" Abraham laughed.

Maybe I moved too soon. I didn't want Jacob to know I was there.

Jacob began to sweat. He didn't know what had come over him, but he knew he had no intentions of spending that much on the case. Jacob was just there for his portion of the briefcase's contents. Why did he say that?

"I know you don't have more than seven fifty, Jacob," Abraham stated.

"And what if I do?" Jacob asked with my help.

"You're either walking away with your cut of the deal and the money that I generously offered you, or you're walking away with nothing at all. It's your choice."

"If the kid has the money, let him bid Abe. We're keeping this fair. We all want that briefcase."

I could hear Jacob's thoughts. He knew there was some part of his mind that needed him to buy the briefcase. He didn't know who I was, but he knew I wanted it. And so, he bid.

"One thousand. Or— I guess one billion—," Jacob declared, attempting to sound triumphant.

"I'm out," Isaac said.

Abraham gave Jacob a death glare. "I'm supposed to believe you have one billion dollars?"

"Yes," Jacob said.

"Fine. I'm out too. But I'm watching you wire the money before you even touch that case," Abraham said.

"That's fair," Jacob replied.

"Let's get our shares out now," Abraham said to Isaac.

Abraham pulled the briefcase towards himself, opening it and pulling out a manila envelope. He took out a document, looking over the first page and smiling, before putting it back.

Isaac went next, pulling out a small velvet box with a ring inside, perhaps a diamond. He lifted the ring towards the ceiling, the light from the lightbulb refracting through the shiny ring. Carefully, Isaac put the ring back in its box.

"Jacob, you're up next," Isaac said.

"I'm going to wait to open it," Jacob replied. "I'll have time when I'm back home."

-o-o-o-

It was raining when Jacob walked out of the building, briefcase in hand. He stepped over a puddle to reach the limousine parked in front. His chauffeur held the door open for him, then quickly walked to the driver's seat to avoid being drenched.

Now that I had gotten him to purchase the briefcase, the first part of my plan was complete.

"I need to make a quick stop!" I said through Jacob.

"Where do you need to stop?" the chauffeur asked.

"There's a bar called The Outlook. I need to meet someone there," I said.

"Sir, I hate to ask, but aren't you getting near three months sober? Are you sure you want to—" *the chauffeur began to say before I cut him off.*

"This is a big day. I'm celebrating," I snapped.

"It's just" This isn't like you, sir. You were making real progress."

"Do I need a new chauffeur?"

"I'm sorry, sir. We'll head there straight away."

I rolled up the divider between Jacob and the chauffeur. Jacob was confused, but he remained oblivious. He still thought he was in control. He didn't understand that I had power over him.

Jacob was rather unintelligent. I'm not entirely sure how I ended up with him as a vessel. I'd been stuck as a passive observer in his brain ever since the day he was born and only recently learned to take control.

Jacob had a wealthy family and lived his life taking advantage of their money. He never made good choices.

The first time I took control, he had spent the night drinking and was trying to drive home. The idiot nearly drove off a bridge. At the last possible second, I worked up the courage to intervene by steering him back onto the road. I don't know what would've happened if he'd died and I'd done nothing.

That's when I realized, after being a passive observer in the back of his mind, I could take small amounts of control. I also realized that when he was drunk, it became easier to take over. Maybe it was because he was in an altered mindset. When he went out to parties, I was able to live my life through him.

After a while, I started getting better at using him as a vessel, and I was beginning to get the hang of controlling him while he was sober.

Then, his pretentious mother threatened to cut off his cash flow if he didn't stop his 'little drinking habit,' and it became more difficult for me to control him. So, I waited. Gathering my energy. After observing his life for so long,

I knew the importance of the briefcase, and I knew I needed it if I was ever going to have full power over him.

The briefcase was the key to my plan.

The limousine slowed to a halt. We were at the bar, and Jacob finally clued in. He wanted to get up or speak, but he couldn't move his arms or legs. To him, it felt like one of those nightmares where you try to scream, but nothing comes out. He was terrified his parents would catch him drinking again. In his mind, he was pleading with the chauffeur to drive him back home.

I walked out of the car and took out the briefcase. I slammed the door shut behind me. I looked up at the fluorescent 'The Outlook' sign and noticed the lights in the letter 'k' had burnt out.

The place desperately needed renovations.

Inside the bar, there were very few customers. I immediately recognized the bartender and went over to talk to him.

"What's the strongest drink you've got?" I asked.

"Not even gonna say hello, Jacob?" the bartender asked.

"Hello. I want to be drunk. Give me alcohol," I replied.

"Fine. Give me a minute," the bartender said.

I let go. If I couldn't get Jacob drunk, I'd lose my power over him. At this point, though, I realized I didn't need to be in command – Jacob would probably get drunk himself.

Jacob sat on the barstool, waiting for the drink. He reached into his pocket and pulled out his phone, scrolling through dozens of emails without actually reading any of them. *He was nervous.*

The bartender placed a drink on the table in front of Jacob. Trembling, Jacob reached for it, the feeling of the ice-cold glass in his hand familiar but oddly awkward. Suddenly, he dropped the drink, spilling it on the table, the floor, and his lap.

"The hell was that, man?" the bartender said as he turned to see the spill.

Jacob didn't reply. Instead, he grabbed his phone again and scrolled through his contacts to the name Anatta Balliol– a kind lady he met at his AA meetings. She picked up his call immediately.

Jacob placed some cash on the table, grabbed the briefcase, and quickly left the bar. He was stuttering into the phone about losing control and how he wanted to be a better person. *It was all nonsense.*

His chauffeur was waiting in the car. Once he noticed Jacob stepping out of the bar, he walked around and opened his door.

Jacob stared at him for a second, the rain still pouring down. He could feel each drop. Anatta was trying to calm him down from the other side of the phone.

This idiot was about to ruin my whole plan. I used my energy to throw the phone to the ground. It landed next to a puddle on the concrete. Thank God Jacob never got a phone case. It broke on impact.

"I think you should head home, sir. Here let me help you in," the chauffer began.

"Take me home, and if I tell you to bring me anywhere else, do not listen to me," Jacob told the chauffeur. "I'm not in the right frame of mind."

Jacob picked up his phone and sat in the backseat. He attempted to dry it off and power it back on, but it was ruined.

Jacob was drenched from the rain, sitting in the back of his limousine, ruining the leather seat. He stared into space for a moment and then began to sob.

The briefcase was sitting on the car floor. I still had a chance. I had to wait, though. I let Jacob cry, knowing he'd give in eventually.

-o-O-o-

Three days after Jacob bought the briefcase, I had enough energy to intervene again. Jacob had been compulsively checking inside of the case to ensure it was the real thing. Other than a rushed checkup with his therapist, he hadn't left it alone.

I was holding back, waiting for my opportunity.

Jacob was sitting on his bed next to the briefcase. He lifted it onto his lap and flicked open the golden latches with shaking hands.

The inside of the briefcase was pitch black, impossible to illuminate. No matter how much light shone in, the contents of the case were hidden by shadows.

There was an engraving on the side of the briefcase. It stated, "**This case holds your greatest desire.**"

It was true. The case really did hold the greatest desire of whoever reached inside. When I first heard of it, I assumed it was a simple lie. I thought someone was trying to trick Jacob out of his parent's money. Of course, he believed them without proof. At least he was lucky. He joined a group trying to steal the briefcase from Ogdenville's newest billionaire. I never expected the case would actually work, and I certainly never expected Jacob, of all people, could get away with stealing it.

I wonder what he thought he would get from it? What Jacob's greatest desire was? Knowing him, he'd probably find some way to pull a luxury car out of the briefcase. Or maybe, if he were lucky, the briefcase would let him pull out something that would make his parents proud of him. Though, I doubt it could perform miracles that astounding.

All I had to do was wait for Jacob to reach into the case and take control. My one desire was an escape from his vessel. I didn't know how it'd form, but when I reached into the case, I knew I'd be a step closer.

Jacob shut the case before I had a chance to react. He didn't even reach inside. Shit. Why did he start to resist vice only when I was nearing escape?

Jacob grabbed his home phone and called the woman he met at his AA meetings.

"Hello?"

"Hi, Anatta."

"Jacob! What happened? Your call cut off a few days ago. I've been calling non-stop. You scared me!"

"Don't worry, it's okay, I'm okay."

"What happened, Jacob?"

"I went to a bar."

"Oh no. Did you drink?"

"No, of course not. But I almost did. It scared me. It felt like there was something else there. There was something that had some sort of power over me. I don't know. I sound crazy."

"It's okay, Jacob. Sometimes life can feel like that. You took control, though – you didn't drink! That's a sign that you're doing way better than the Jacob I met three months ago."

"It felt like something else took over, though. I've felt that a lot lately. It's terrifying. I don't understand what's going on."

"Jacob, you need to remember. You have control. You can take control. Next time you feel like that, you need to stand your ground. Don't let your impulses get the better of you-"

I hung up the phone, then threw it to the ground. I couldn't let Jacob hear any more of that bullshit. I turned Jacob towards the briefcase again and pried it open. The two latches broke off.

The black void in the briefcase was as devoid of light as ever. I reached inside.

Jacob was fighting back, trying to overcome me, but he was weak. I pushed back, reaching into the void and pulled out my greatest desire.

Jacob pulled what he thought to be his greatest desire out of the briefcase. *A bottle of tequila.*

"No," Jacob muttered to himself.

He reached into the briefcase again.

I retook control.

Jacob pulled out another bottle.

Was this the only way for me to take control? By keeping him drunk forever? My one desire was to escape from Jacob, not keeping him drunk and living disguised as his impulses.

Or was the briefcase trying to give me some sort of reminder? Could this be a symbol? Jacob drank Tequila that night when he nearly drove off a bridge. That was the source of my power. The first time I had power. I intervened and saved his life.

What if I didn't stop him?

What if that was what the briefcase was trying to tell me?

Jacob took a long sip from the bottle.

He let a few tears flow out.

Took a few more sips.

Then decided the briefcase was wrong.

This wasn't what he wanted.

He picked up his phone, called the chauffeur, and told him to take the day off.

He walked out to his car.

He threw the briefcase in the back seat.

And drove to Anatta's house.

Solitary Confinement

I sat up in my cell. I was alone this time. Usually, I had at least one other person stuck with me, but now, the cell was barren. Even more than usual. The walls were painted white. All the cell held was a bed with matching white sheets, a bookshelf holding only blank books, and a toilet. They must have transferred me somewhere new. Probably somewhere deeper in the heart of The Orb. I was getting bored, so when the guard showed up to bring me my lunch, I put him in a chokehold. He shot me, and everything started over again.

The Walls Have Eyes

Subject: **Important!**

From: account12279@nicemail.rem

To: pi.jbwaltz@email.com

> Hello J. B. Waltz,
>
> I'd like to keep this email anonymous. I have a case that I need help with. I can't investigate it on my own anymore. Given your reputation, I was hoping you could help.
>
> Someone I care about was kidnapped. I'm a detective working under the local police department and, despite my connection to the victim, the chief assigned me to the case. You may have heard about it. The case had some mainstream coverage when it first broke, but it's been fading out of the news cycle lately. May Contreras. We've been after the kidnapper for almost a month, and we were finally catching up to him. That was until we were ordered to stop investigating.
>
> New leads were coming in daily. We even received a letter from the kidnapper. He's one of those types that sends cryptic coded BS. God knows why. He

probably saw a movie about the Zodiac Killer and thought of the killer as an idol.

The case was progressing well before we were told to stop. Ever since the department was brought under 'new management,' we've been banned from working on the case. They deemed it a 'waste of funds.' About a dozen other cases have taken the same treatment—all with the same excuse.

I don't trust what's going on right now. Some billionaire BOUGHT the police force, and now we aren't allowed to investigate a dozen cases due to funds? It just doesn't add up.

To get to the point, I'm sending you this because the chief'll fire me if I get caught investigating on my own. I don't have much money to pay you, but if you manage to figure anything out, I could scrape a bit together.

I've attached all the case files I could get my hands on.

Please, help us.

- M.A.

P. S. If you need to contact me, you can email me back here for the next twenty-four hours, but I will not reply. After twenty-four hours, I will be deleting this account. If you agree to help me, I can bring you a burner phone. On the back, I'll leave you a note with an untraceable number where you can contact me. If the guy stopping us from working on this case paid you off, or if you're on their side or anything like that, don't try to figure out who I am. I'm sure you'll find it's near impossible.

Subject: **Re: Important!**

From: pi.jbwaltz@email.com

To: account12279@nicemail.rem

Hello Marco Aquinos,

You were an easy man to track down, but you don't need to worry about me being on 'their side.' You told me your initials, the fact that you're on the police force, and that you worked on the May Contreras case. Anyone could figure out your identity from that email with a few minutes of research. I recommend destroying your computer's hard drive, just to be safe.

The case you forwarded me is intriguing, and it seems the incompetent people at the station are even more worthless now. I'll help you, but I need you to follow my orders. You need to send me every piece of information you have. You mentioned the kidnapper sent a letter to the police force. I'll need that too.

Out of curiosity, what were you planning to do with a burner phone? Give it to one of my secretaries? You couldn't have my address, so I'm assuming you simply lack foresight.

I will have a burner phone delivered to you. I suggest you start saving the files I request on thumb drives and emailing them to me from public library computers in different cities. I'd recommend Pacrown, Royal Landwith, Jonestead, Ogdenville, and Oxton, in that order. In each library, make sure no one is following you. I have people working for me at each of the five locations. If you make any mistakes, they will notify me, and you will lose all contact. You won't need to contact me five times, though. I'll solve the case by then.

Don't make any mistakes.

-J. B. Waltz

Notes

Can I trust Marco Aquinos? His identity was suspiciously easy to figure out. Either he's an idiot, or he is not who he claims to be. The files he shared with me seem to be missing sections. This isn't the whole picture.

FILE 1-A, May's online activity leading up to her disappearance:

-o-o-o-

🔍 **https://www.homeowners.forums.rem**

~o~HomeOwner's Forum~o~

Please, read the forum rules before posting.

Strange Noises from Inside the Walls?

Posted May 15th

4:01 PM

User: MayFlowers1992

Hi Everyone! My name is May! I live alone in a small two-room house (my roommate is in the process of moving out now). I spend most of my time painting in my bedroom, which is across the hall from my roommate's room. She's emptied almost everything from there, but recently I've been hearing loud creaking noises coming from her room. The noises started recently, and maybe I'm just paranoid, but it's starting to concern me.

I went to her room to check, and I realized the creaking sound was coming from inside of the walls. I guess my question is, are noises from inside of the wall normal? Could I have a plumbing issue? Is something else wrong?

Comments (3):

User: *g.rave.yard.22*   @ *05/15 4:22 PM*

I've had this kind of issue before. From what I understand, the temperature can affect the pipes in your home – make them contract and expand. It's all pretty standard stuff. You get used to it after a while.

User: *dontemailmedavid*   @ *05/15 5:07 PM*

Houses make noises. This isn't anything that matters.

User: **[account deleted]**   @ *05/15 11:22 PM*

Did your roommate leave on good terms? Who knows? She could've been a witch.

-o-o-o-

Strange Noises from Inside the Walls? [Update]

Posted May 17th

2:27 AM

User: *MayFlowers1992*

Hi! This is just an update to my last post **_here_**. I woke up about an hour ago to a loud thud in my roommates' room. At first, I shouted to my roommate to keep it down, but then my mind connected the dots. She had moved out. Nothing and no one should be in there.

I got scared, so I took out a flashlight from my bedside drawer and a baseball bat from my closet. I used to play a lot when I was younger, so I still had it lying around. I flicked the light on and tried to creep out of my room and across the hall silently. If something was in there, it could probably hear me hyperventilating. I heard another bang, louder than the first. With a burst of adrenaline, I pushed the door open.

The room was the same as I had left it, but there was a massive crack in the wall. Water was dripping through the apartment's thin drywall. I'm assuming a pipe burst or something. I'm going to call a plumber soon, but is there anything I should do in the meantime?

I've been shaking for the last hour, worried someone was in my apartment with me, but now that I've been awake for a little while, I've calmed down.

Comments (1):

User: *alwaysondrm77*   @ *05/17 9:22 AM*

I had that happen at my old summer house. Something clogged the pipe, and it just burst. Cost me almost a thousand bucks to replace. Just put some towels down and see if it's still a problem in a week before you call anyone. Good luck.

🔍 **https://www.arthelp.forums.rem**

~o~The Art Help Forum~o~

A friendly place to share your art, ask for advice, and more!

Paint Recommendations?

Posted May 18th

2:10 PM

User: MayFlowers1992

Hello! There have been a few leaks in my house recently. First, a pipe in my old roommate's room burst, and now one in my room burst. I saved most of my paintings, thankfully! :)! I did, however, lose a lot of supplies. Some canvases, pastels, and all my paints! I came here to ask everyone what art supplies they use, so I could choose some new things for myself.

For an example of my regular work, click ***here***! It's one of my older paintings. It's the silhouette of a boy holding an umbrella at sundown. I liked the colours in this one, but it was so long ago I don't even remember which paints I used.

Comments (2):

User: ***[account deleted]***　　　　@ *05/18 4:52 PM*

　　　I use blood to paint like a real artist. You should too.

User: slowpicasso.111　　　　@ *05/18 5:02 PM*

　　　Here's a *link* to a shopping list with some of my favourite materials! I hope you enjoy it!

-o-o-o-

Compiled by Officer Daniels 06/22

Initially, I suspected that the shopping list link was secretly tracking May, but after further investigation, that theory proved to be false.

Note to self: Ask "Marco Aquinos" what the deleted account's usernames were...

File 3-A, May Contreras' email log.

-o-o-o-

Subject Line: **Updates**

From: mayflowers1992@email.rem

To: marcia.contreras.1949@email.rem

>Hi Mom,
>
>I hope you're doing well at home! I've been doing great! I have buyers lined up for my art. It's selling faster than I can paint it! :) I just wanted to let you know that you don't have to worry! I'm doing perfectly fine.
>
>Love you lots,
>
>May

Subject Line: **Invoice [Reply]**

From: mayflowers1992@email.rem

Replying To: plumbingdonewright@email.rem

>Hello again,
>
>Thanks for sending me the invoice so soon. I'm just curious, what does it mean by external damage fee? Wasn't the damage caused by the pipe clogging up

on the inside? Either way, I might need a little while to pay for this. Is there any way I can pay you guys in a month or so? I already had to turn off my phone service a few weeks ago, and if possible, I'd like to pay you guys back without taking out another loan.

Thanks again,

May

Subject Line: **Invoice [Reply] [Reply]**

From: plumbingdonewright@email.rem

Replying To: mayflowers1992@email.rem

Hi May,

A few responses for you. First off, we can defer your payment for up to a week at most. Secondly, that external damage fee means what you'd think. Someone took a real hard swing at those pipes. Party too hard, maybe? lol

Anyways, we look forward to hearing from you again soon,

Jim Wright

Subject Line: **Plumbing Issues**

From: mayflowers1992@email.rem

To: bubbleyhearts266@nicemail.rem

> Hi Reyna,
>
> Any chance you know about the plumbing issues in the apartment? I know you already left, but the guy I hired said someone hit the pipes. I have no clue how it would have happened, but I'm just wondering if you know anything?
>
> Thanks,
>
> May

Subject: **Painting Techniques [Unread]**

From: mayflowers1992@email.rem

To: mayflowers1992@email.rem

> Have you tried my method yet? I think it'd help you become a true artist. xoxoxo

Subject: **Please Reply**

From: mayflowers1992@email.rem

To: bubbleyhearts266@nicemail.rem

Hi Reyna,

Can you please talk to me? It's okay if you were involved somehow in damaging the pipes. It just seems like you've been avoiding contact with me. I noticed you only came to pick up your things while I was out. Could you please tell me why?

Did I do something?

I'm sorry,

May.

Subject: **What Did I do?**

From: mayflowers1992@email.rem

To: bubbleyhearts266@nicemail.rem

Hi Reyna,

I'm starting to worry. Is there something I did that made you leave? I'm not worried about the pipes, if that's it. I found the hole in the wall behind my bookcase, though. I seriously won't hold this against you. I just want answers. Was this you? I'm finding new things every day, and honestly, it's starting to worry me.

Please message me back.

Subject: **Autoreply**

From: services-auto-reply@nicemail.rem

To: mayflowers1992@email.rem

Hi mayflowers1992!

Sorry for the inconvenience, but it appears the email address *bubbleyhearts266@nicemail.rem* does not exist. Either the email address never existed, or the user has deleted it.

Just in case, double-check your spelling! If you think this is an error, please contact us **here.**

-o-0-o-

The idea that the killer was inside of May's home is haunting, but it only deepens my curiosity. What point was there in sending an email from May's computer? If it was to scare her, it never worked because May didn't see it. There are still pieces missing from this puzzle. I need all of them before I can put the criminal's actions together.

The following is a letter received by the Ogdenville police department. Police found the letter to have May Contreras' fingerprints on it. There were no other fingerprints.

Was she forced to write this letter at gunpoint? Did she fake her kidnapping? Or was her kidnapper just smart enough to wear gloves and have May handle it?

The Letter

"I will follow my saviour as long as he stands-

He became God to

guide us to salvat

ion The poor girl-

//

He told me what I needed to do to save her.

He promises me it's important for the coming

of the new age- but it seems so cruel Oh well

//

Obedience to the new God will save our souls-

He brings wealth.

He brings love-

He brings power-"

Even the police think they've figured this one out. "SAVE OUR SOULS" is a phrase commonly expressed in Morse code. The police started looking at the dots, periods, and dashes throughout the letter. Based on the spacing of each paragraph, the dots and dashes spell out a simple answer.

-- // .- // -.--   = M // A // Y

The kidnapper spelt out May's name in Morse code. I bet the police took themselves out for doughnuts after solving something that "difficult."

This code by itself is utterly useless to the investigation. But I believe it was a decoy. Put simply, that code was noticeable and pointless. The questions that I need to ask about the letter should focus on the intentions behind it.

Why would a kidnapper send a letter to a police station if not to ask for a ransom? It could be a matter of the killer wanting to be famous, like the Zodiac Killer, but there's a flaw in that logic as well. The writer is worshipping a "God." Criminals looking for fame are usually narcissists. Wouldn't you expect him to write about himself as "God"? He gives credit to another person, which would be out of character if his motive was fame.

I think this kidnapper is mocking the police. I believe that there's a secret hidden in these words that the kidnapper will eventually reveal- a significant clue that will be useless by the time they reveal it. Then the kidnapper can claim "the police had the answer in their hands the entire time" and stir civil unrest. Proof that the police are fools.

Then again, that should be common knowledge at this point.

    For now, that's simply a theory. Who knows, the kidnapper could've just been a disgruntled guy with a vendetta.

Lion Mobile Phone Records

"Am I speaking to Marco Aquinos?"

"Yes, you are. Now, who are you? Who is calling, and why are you synthesizing your speech? I can barely understand what you're saying."

"I am known as J. B. Waltz to you."

"I should have figured. What are you doing to your voice?"

"I have to hide my voice, so you don't recognize me if I ever need to speak with you in person."

"It's good to know you trust me."

"Don't be sarcastic. Let's get straight to the point. I need you to send me more information."

"Again? Christ. What else do you need? I sent you everything on the last two trips."

"In all honesty, I think there's a chance you may be the kidnapper."

"Excuse me?"

"To be fair, it's only a small chance."

"What makes me suspicious?"

"Well, when I thought about who you could be, I figured the only person with all of this information would be a police officer or the kidnapper. Someone with a vendetta against me trying to trick me into some sort of trap where you could kill me."

"That entire idea is crazy- I'm an officer. I can show you my ID! You're the one who figured out who I was."

"It was suspiciously easy to figure out. Go to the Royal Landwith library and talk to the guy at the front desk. Show him your police ID and tell him to contact Owen Silvera."

"Who is Owen Silvera?"

"Me. I don't give out my real name to anyone. Now go to the library, show the man at the front desk your police ID, and ask him to contact Owen Silvera."

Call Disconnected

It was only a small chance, but I needed to be sure the information Marco gave me was reliable. He was at least willing to listen to me. The tracker I had put on his phone told me he left his house immediately and headed in the library's direction.

My suspicion for him dropped before he even arrived. By following my instructions, I became sure the Marco Aquinos I was in contact with was the real Marco Aquinos. A bit of a shame, though. If he was the kidnapper, it might have made the case much more straightforward.

File 3-B

The following are the notes of Officer Daniels from his interview with Reyna Miller. The notes have been typed for increased readability. Illegible text is marked with [...].

06/20

-o-o-o-

- Reyna lived in the same home as May for three years after finishing high school. May got a mortgage to purchase the home. It was cheap due to the remote location.
- Reyna describes a general change in May's behaviour near the end of their time living together.
- Reyna began to find her belongings painted red. It started with her wallet and slowly grew to her phone's screen being painted over.
- In the days leading up to her moving out, Reyna discovered paint was being mixed into the drinks she kept in the fridge.
- When confronted, May claimed she would never touch Reyna's belongings without permission.
- Reyna didn't want to argue and instead packed her things to move out.
- Reyna claims she never opened May's emails and instead deleted her email address to avoid future contact.

- Reyna claims to know nothing about the damaged pipes, the hole behind the bookshelf, or the evidence discovered earlier today (see attached descriptors).

Reyna claims not to recognize the following pieces of evidence discovered before her interview at 11:20 AM on 06/20. Police discovered this evidence in a hidden compartment between the walls in Contreras' apartment. Information here is a summarized copy of the information provided in folder 7-E.

7-E-6: 2TB Camera

-A camera holding hours of footage of May sleeping. The footage appears to have been filmed without her knowledge. Often heavy breathing can be heard from the other side of the recording.

7-E-7: 6x6 Business Card

-A business card for an art convention. Discovered next to the camera.

-Front text:

"THE MILLENNIUM ART CONVENTION!

Come view the work of countless incredibly talented artists or submit your artwork for display!"

-Back text:

"To buy tickets or submit art for display, please contact us at:

milleniumartconvention@freemail.rem

+1-(555)-809-4545

282 Alsberry Street – Millennium Convention Center."

"*July 30th / May*" was written on the back of the card in red pen. The street number '282' was crossed out, and the letters 'SOS' was written in its place.

7-E-11: Notebook

Found in the hidden compartment. 6.5x10 cover. Flowers on the front. All the pages were blank except for the first five. Sketches of a woman dancing, noticeably different features from May.

-o-o-o-

I think the business card is the key to solving the code from the kidnapper's letters. The kidnapper had a clear plan but likely didn't expect the privatization of the police force.

It's clear now that he left these objects behind intentionally. This is the same person that wrote the coded letter to the police. He isn't stupid enough to make a mistake like leaving a business card with a specific date, time, and location at the crime scene unless it's a trick of some sort.

I get it. The kidnapper plans to embarrass the police force by committing murder on the same street the police are going to camp out on- the art exhibit is a distraction, and the code that police never looked past holds the correct address!

Of course, that's just a slight possibility, and I can't jump to conclusions. Yet. First, I need to look past the decoy code in the kidnapper's letter and see what I can find.

"I will follow my saviour as long as he stands-

He became God to

guide us to salvat

ion The poor girl-

//

He told me what I needed to do to save her.

He promises me it's important for the coming

of the new age- but it seems so cruel Oh well

//

Obedience to the new God will save our souls-

He brings wealth.

He brings love-

He brings power-"

The structure of the sentences bothers me the most. The alternating between long and short sentences...

That's it!

- . . . // - - - // - . . .

That spells out: B // O // B

A strange answer to the code, but that must be it. The long sentences represent dashes, and the short sentences represent dots.

But what relevance does BOB have? I expected a numerical value to come out of this that would link to an address on Alsberry – the same street as the convention center.

That theory may be inaccurate, but there must be some relevance to this code.

. - - - // . . . // . - - -

J // S // J

If I assume longer sentences represent dots, then JSJ becomes the relevant code. There's something I'm missing. There's another piece to this puzzle that hasn't been found yet. Or am I looking for something that isn't there?

If I use the common alpha-numeric code A=1, Z=26, perhaps I can work from the solution back to the code.

If JSJ is the correct code, then the address would have to be 101910 Alsberry street.

If BOB is the correct code, then the address would have to be 2152 Alsberry street.

With a bit of research, I can quickly find out that Alsberry street ends on the number 2152. This is the first detail that makes the code feel like less of a coincidence. It's an abandoned home.

I need to figure out the value of these numbers. What is the point of the code? Is my theory still valid? Has it been three nights since the last time I slept? There are only two days until July 30th. I can wait.

I think May Contreras is going to be murdered on July 30th at 2152 Alsberry Street, and I'm pretty sure there's only one police officer that's willing to help me.

2152 Alsberry Street - Transcript

"Marco, are you filming this?"

"Of course, Waltz, despite what you say, I'm not an idiot."

"I never said you were an idiot, Marco; I only implied it. Let's go."

Marco Aquinos lifted the camera and pointed it at 2152 Alsberry Street.

Alsberry was a strange street. It nearly ran through the entire city. One end of the street ran downtown, attached to the convention center, hotels, clubs, clothing stores, and all the other neon-signed buildings. The other end of the street ran through a residential neighbourhood. The kind you wouldn't take a second look at. A street with innocence. Kids were out playing hockey in the sun and running to the sidewalk every time someone shouted "car." Neighbours were holding polite conversation. Despite this, on the very same innocent street, a private detective and a man he didn't trust were standing outside of an abandoned home that was soon to be a crime scene.

2152 Alsberry street was at the far end of the residential area. It appeared as if the grass hadn't been mowed in ages. It stuck out like a sore thumb in a neighbourhood that seemed perfect.

Marco walked up from the driveway, holding the camera with one hand. He knocked on the door, but there was no answer.

"I've got this," Waltz said as he reached his hand out to the brass doorknob. "See, it was unlocked. I knew it would be unlocked."

"How would you know something like that?" Marco turned the camera to face Waltz.

"Just trust me."

The two walked into the seemingly abandoned home together. The floorboards creaked as they walked through. It looked like some kids had broken in at some point. Someone etched a heart into the decrepit wall with the words 'lock + key' written in the centre. Probably some young teenage couple with weird nicknames.

"Are you sure this isn't breaking and entering or anything like that? We don't have a warrant. I think we should back out." Marco was sweating, but the house had a cool breeze.

"The police aren't pursuing this case anymore. You're off duty. I'm a private investigator. Think about it, realistically. If my deductions are correct, there's probably some ulterior motive involving whoever bought out the police force. I'm not looking into that yet, but it's important to keep in mind. The justice system is rigged, and whoever's responsible for this won't face charges. All we can do to help is save the kidnapped girl."

"You think the police were privatized to cover this up? Isn't that a little unlikely?"

"There's a lot of reasons behind that privatization, Marco, but I think- actually- I'd say it's incredibly likely that the person behind the privatization is the same person the kidnapper is calling God."

Marco felt something metal press against the back of his head. "Don't move. Either of you," a voice called from behind Marco and Waltz.

"What are your names?"

"Marco." "Waltz."

"Are you holding any weapons?"

"Nope." "No."

"Drop the camera."

The camera fell from Marco's hands and hit the ground with a thud.

"I thought the person that'd crack my code would be smart enough to not walk in empty-handed," the man, presumably the kidnapper, said. He had a gravelly voice.

"Why did you leave a code?" Waltz turned around, despite the kidnapper holding a gun to Marco's head.

"What's that, Wally?" the kidnapper asked.

"My name is Waltz. Why did you leave a code for the police?"

"To be honest, I just thought it'd make the police look like even bigger idiots than we all already know they are. I guess it also doubled as a trap for anyone smart enough to figure it out."

"And why did you kidnap May?" Waltz wasn't breaking eye contact with the kidnapper.

"This isn't an interview, Waltz, just give this guy what he wants so we can get out of here." Marco could feel his heart beating rapidly. Adrenaline was coursing through his veins, but all he could do was stand still.

"Marky, that wouldn't be as much fun. Walt, to answer your question, I do everything to appease my God."

"Who is your God?"

"He doesn't tell us his real name, but he's shown me his powers. He brought my wife back from the dead." The kidnapper grinned.

"And how did he do that?"

"I listened to what he told me to do, and one day he brought me a briefcase."

"A briefcase?"

"He told me to take what was inside the briefcase, then give the case back to him. It was a beautiful case, so I understand why he wanted to keep it."

"What was inside of it?"

"There was a letter. It was from her. She talked about things only she could have known about. Our first dance, when we ditched prom together, our honeymoon. Nobody else could've written it."

"Was that all?"

"Well, the letter had an address and a time in it. It was a run-down convenience store. My wife- Hey! What-"

While Waltz was talking, a woman silently walked into the home. She surprised the kidnapper with a pistol against the back of his head.

"Drop it," she said.

The kidnapper dropped his weapon, and the woman quickly restrained his hands. She took out an object that looked like a pen and stuck it into the man's arm. After a few seconds, he fell unconscious.

"I see you've met my stand-in, Andre," she said. "You know me as J.B. Waltz."

"The hell is going on?" Marco asked, shocked.

"Don't worry about that for now, just trust us. You have handcuffs on you, right?" Andre asked.

"Yeah, here," Marco said, handing the handcuffs to Andre. He couldn't stop staring at the kidnapper, who was slumped on the floor. "What's- what is happening?"

"Well, I'm the real Waltz," she said, "and that's Andre. Of course, to protect our identities, we use different names, but he's my assistant."

"Huh? Why did he tell me he was Waltz?" Marco asked.

"He was playing a role. I didn't know if we could fully trust you, Marco, and this house was essentially a death trap. I can't believe you agreed to walk into it without knowing of any backup."

"You put him to sleep too early, though, J. B.," Andre said. "He was just starting to give us useful info."

"We have time for that when he wakes up. For now, we need to check on May."

"P24102!" A voice shouted, "Wake up!"

"I'll check for her upstairs. You check downstairs."

"I said wake up!"

"May? Are you there?"

"Wake up or I'll have you executed again, just for the fun of it."

"She's down here!"

The Curse of a Past Life

Sometimes they change my cell. Other times they change my form. This time, when I woke up, I was in the same barren cell as before but in a different body, probably in my mid to late twenties. I've been through countless forms with each death, so this is nothing new to me. The prison guard dropped my lunch off again, but I didn't feel like a reset yet. I noticed a small crack in the cell wall. It wasn't much, but it was something new. I must have done something right in my previous life to earn such a helpful escape route.

I took the tray from the guard and even forced out a polite smile. I kept getting the exact same meal. Corn, rice, potatoes, and chicken. They didn't even have the decency to give us seasoning. I sat the tray on my bed and took the fork and knife towards the crack in the wall. I didn't have the determination to spend nineteen years digging like the guy from *Shawshank*, but I was at least willing to make a quick attempt. I jammed the knife into the crack and pushed to try and remove one of the stones. The knife snapped in half.

Out of frustration,

I kicked the wall. There was a

deafeningly loud, low-pitched noise. The crack

quickly ran up towards the ceiling. Oh no. The guards

probably heard it. I rushed to push the bookcase in front of

the cracked wall as a guard showed up in front of my cell.

"The hell was that?" he shouted. I was at a loss for words.

I don't think he saw the crack in the wall, but there

was no way to hide the noise. I jumped towards

him, and he drew his weapon firing

at me through the cell bars.

Wealth of Blood

"Alright, Scarlett, whenever you're ready," one of the ten investors that lined the table said to me. They were some of the first people I would ever tell my story to. Other than my mother and my research team, of course.

"It all started with me trying to save a cat," I began, "I was twelve years old and watched in horror as a car struck the poor thing. It was one of the worst sights of my life. I was a dumb kid, so I ran into the middle of the road towards the cat, tears in my eyes.

A car quickly braked to avoid hitting me, but I barely noticed. I stood, looking at the cat, just barely clinging to life, when I felt something strange.

I had a scrape on my knee from earlier. It was still bleeding, but I had been ignoring it. Again, I was an incredibly dumb kid." There was a slight murmur in the room.

"Out of nowhere, the blood from my knee was pulled towards the cat like some kind of magic, and there was light coming from the cat's wounds. In less than a minute, its injuries had seemed to heal entirely. I picked up the cat and brought him back to the sidewalk.

He was a black cat, very fluffy, and he didn't have a collar. I tried to send him off, but he kept following me everywhere I went.

By some miracle of fate, I was able to convince my parents to let us keep him. We took him to the vet, got his fur trimmed, and searched for weeks but couldn't find his original owner. Eventually, we named him Liquorice.

I spent the next few days trying to test out my new 'superpowers.' I went on hikes every day looking for an injured animal to help. I kept a piece of glass in my pocket, just in case I needed to draw blood and use my healing abilities.

Eventually, I found a bird that looked like it had a broken wing. I took the shard of glass and nervously drew a few drops of blood from my palm.

It happened again. My blood was pulled towards the bird, and the light shined out again. It was healed, and I was amazed.

That was all when I was only twelve years old. Now, I have created a product that will bring humanity to its maximum potential."

The investors sitting around the table had strange looks on their faces. They seemed not to believe me.

"Trust me when I say my blood can cure everything. It can cure any disease; it'll even reverse ageing. I've been working with a team of scientists over the last few years to figure out how to maximize the amount of blood that could be harvested without harming me, and the results are astounding.

Now, I know some of you don't believe me, but just watch this. I've got someone coming in to demonstrate. She's my neighbour, and her name is Edna – she's a real angel."

I stepped into the hall and asked Edna to come inside.

"If I just take a drop of blood and place it on her tongue like this…"

The blood was magnetized towards Edna before it even left the eyedropper. Beams of light began to shine out of her, and the wrinkles in her skin began to fade. The people sitting around the table gasped and mumbled with excitement.

"There we go! Just like that, she looks fifteen years younger." The investors applauded. Some of them stared in disbelief. Another took their glasses off to take another look.

"Now, I just need some strong financial help to share this cure with the world. Trust me, what I gave Edna is only the beginning of what it can do. I need someone to help supply the money to bring this all-curing, age-reversing product to the public."

Everyone in the room was excited. They didn't know what was to come.

-o-o-o-

I have this recurring dream. It's serene. In the dream, I live on top of a mountain in a small, quiet home. Nobody bothers me there. I make art out of coloured sand, I take care of the animals that find their way to my home, and once a week, I walk down to town to donate blood.

I don't understand how any real person could live like that. It's too quiet. I'd probably turn it into a re-enactment of *The Shining* if it were real. I probably wouldn't be able to get electricity out there either.

Plus, donating blood once a week? That'd barely help anyone. I understand why some people wouldn't see it that way, but by monetizing my blood, I can spread it to more people. Still, the dream was peaceful, even if it didn't align with my goals in life.

-o-o-o-

Liquorice has probably taken over my alarm clock's job. I guess since he has been with me for twenty years, he's figured out my sleep schedule. He started making noise at six AM, like usual, until I brought him his food.

It had been almost a year since my initial meeting with investors, and they were prepping to launch the blood as an over-the-counter all-disease-curing drug. My life's work was nearly complete.

By the time I made it to the office, journalists and TV crews had already filled the room. I had to push my way past them even to make it to the lunch hall. Some people were working together to set up a projector. This would be my first time seeing the commercial.

It's kind of weird, y'know, seeing a commercial about selling your own blood. I've been working with it my whole life, but it was strange to picture someone walking into a pharmacy and buying a watered-down vial of my blood. Of course, no one knew it was blood except for my team. If word got out, who knows what could've happened. Someone would be bound to try and kidnap me or worse.

One of the investors, an older guy, named Loch, sat next to me while everyone was setting up.

"You're insanely lucky. You know that, right?" he asked.

"I guess so. I just want to help people," I replied.

"Yeah, but you're going to get rich as shit!" he said with a wide grin.

"I just want to help people," I told him.

"I get it, you gotta keep your mask on with all the PR around. I wouldn't want anyone to overhear. Don't worry, I can read between the lines," he replied.

"That's not true. I don't care about money. I want to expand the research and help people," I said in a serious tone with only a slight crack in my voice.

He just nodded and laughed.

Before I had a chance to correct him again, the lights began to dim, and the projector flickered on. An announcement called out for everyone to take their seats and quiet down.

The commercial began to play. A bottle labelled "LYNKSOL" flashed on the screen. Thank God they listened when I said I didn't want my name to be attached to the project. They would've named it Scarlettol or something. Not like the name Lynksol was any catchier, though.

"Now introducing Lynksol! An all-in-one cure for any form of disease. You name it, Lynksol cures it! It can even reverse ageing," the commercial said. "Let's ask Edna, one of our happy customers!"

"Well, today is my eightieth birthday, but after taking just a few drops of Lynksol, well, you can see for yourself," said Edna, who didn't look a day past twenty.

"But that's not all," the commercial continued, "Lynksol is one of the only treatments with no discovered negative side effects. There hasn't been any small text hidden out of view for this entire commercial!"

"Call your local pharmacy! Lynksol is available now in limited quantities."

The commercial seemed strange to me, but the people around me cheered lightly.

I left early. Something about the entire thing didn't sit right with me. It was something about Loch's comments. I mean – it wasn't like I was charging exorbitant prices; I was just trying to make enough money to fund some more research hopefully. Part of me feels strange knowing that some people won't get life-saving treatment because of how much I charge for my medicine, but I could theoretically help more people in the long run this way.

I went to the lab and had one of the workers take some of my blood. I never really got used to the needles. I did get better at recovering, though. I don't get as lightheaded, and I can give a little more blood before, but I felt like we could optimize it further.

I got a ride home and went straight to sleep, feeling more tired this time than before. Maybe it was just stress from the launch. Whatever.

-o-o-o-

The next morning, I slept though both Liquorice trying to wake me up and my alarm clock. It was eight AM, and someone was pounding on my door. I threw on clothes and ran over with Liquorice chasing behind me.

I opened the door to, "Ma'am, I have a delivery to Scarlett Santos from someone named Loch. It says, 'Congrats! We've made it!' Now, can you just sign here?"

The delivery man handed a clipboard to me with a pen attached to it, and I reluctantly signed for the package. A surprisingly large, rectangular cardboard box was wheeled into my room.

"What is it?" I asked.

"I'm not sure, ma'am, I'm just the delivery man," he replied before walking out.

Liquorice ran over to the box and stared at it. I took a pair of scissors from the kitchen and cut the box open at the side. It was a flat-screen television. What the hell?

I think Loch really got the wrong idea. I didn't want this kind of thing. I just wanted to live an average life, and I really hope this didn't come out of money that could have gone towards further research.

Then again, I just accomplished one of my lifelong dreams, and it would be a shame if I didn't at least reward myself a little. I pulled the television out of the box. I wasn't sure where it would fit. I decided to rest it on the floor in front of my bed for the time being.

I didn't have any meetings that day, so I sent Loch a text, asked him why he sent me a television, then plugged everything in, putting on the news.

There was a video of a pharmacy with a line leading out the building and around the block. The news was talking about a miracle drug; the lady reporting called it a gift from the Lord. I knew the product would be a big deal but seeing all the commotion made everything feel real.

Almost every channel I turned to had something about Lynksol on it. From the sounds of it, there were some significant shortages. I needed to give more blood. Now, ~~**Jacob**~~ I usually wasn't supposed to drive so soon after a blood donation, but I'd had enough rest. I could ask one of the interns for a ride home when I was done.

Eventually, after making it through a surprising amount of traffic, I reached the office. I took a few steps in the front door and saw Loch walking down the crowded halls. "Hey, Loch," I shouted as I tried to wave him down. He noticed me and walked over.

"Hey! There's the girl everyone's talking about! How did you like the gift I sent you?" he asked.

"I meant to talk to you about that. I don't want anything like that. Please don't do it again," I said.

"Not even gonna say thank you? I just wanted to give you something as thanks for making us all rich," he replied.

"Rich?" I asked, raising an eyebrow.

"Expect the money to start rolling in soon. It was a major success. I'm getting a new summer home in Florida, and I could use a vacation partner," Loch said.

"I already told you, I want to reinvest in further clinical trials, but have fun alone in Florida, Loch," I replied before walking away.

    I went to the lab and had them take more blood. I was a little dizzy, but I told them it wasn't enough, insisting on them take another sample. I saw a strange grainy pattern that was all different colours. One of the colours looked like a new colour, one I had never seen before. I had to name the new colour, so I called it orange because it was kind of like the colour of the fruit oranges, but it was different from orange as a colour. You know what I'm talking about; you get it, right?

-o-O-o-

  I woke up in the lab with almost a dozen doctors crowded around me. Apparently, I started mumbling gibberish and just passed out. The doctors said I seemed okay when I woke up, and I just needed to take it easy. My memory is a bit foggy, but I think one of the investors came in to see me. It might have been Loch. He looked like a weird cloud.

"Hey, Scarlett, I know you're just waking up, and I hope that doesn't cloud your judgement," the cloud-man began to say.

I interrupted him, "Ha. Cloud my judgement. You're funny."

"Alright then, I guess you're confident, and the doctors say you're stable, so no time like the present. We were planning on introducing a price hike. It's just basic supply and demand. We only have a small amount, so why don't we make the most of it," the ball of gas asked.

"Well, I wanna get a boat!" I think I said.

"That'd be no problem, and we'll get right on it," the cloud-man replied.

  The next part of my weird blood-loss hallucination is hard to remember. I think I woke up in the house on the hill, and the version of me living on top of the hill told me something profound and important. She kept getting mad at me because I didn't understand her until right at the end when I woke up. After actually waking up, I entirely forgot.

Someone from work drove me home. It was one of the doctors. They kept apologizing for taking too much blood. Still, honestly, except for the weird hallucinations and the fact that I faintly remembered something about oranges, I was doing perfectly fine.

-o-o-o-

I woke up in bed the next day and remembered I agreed to a price hike. I was conflicted at first about whether I should go in and demand the price be set back, but honestly, I didn't think I needed to. As long as all of the medicine sold out, I'd still help the same number of people. I'd be helping more people than before because I'd be helping myself and the investors earn money. I could reinvest in furthering my cause. Maybe a price hike might lead to some bad PR, but it'd be fine.

I checked my email and discovered we had a celebratory dinner planned at this fancy restaurant called The Brimstone Kitchen. I had never eaten there in my life, but it sounded interesting. I guess it was also an excellent way to boost everyone's morale after working for so long. The plan seemed somewhat last minute, but it wasn't like I was busy.

I spent the day resting, watching some shows on my new TV, and getting ready for a night out. Then I realized I didn't have clothes that were anywhere near fancy enough for The Brimstone Kitchen. It's the kinda place where you look up the menu online, and they don't even list prices.

I figured I'd probably end up at a few fancy events like this, so it would be a decent idea to buy some nice clothes – purely for the sake of my business. I could be given a bad name or seen as unprofessional if I showed up to a fancy restaurant in regular clothes. So, with a few hours to spare, I stopped by some high-end clothing stores. They were the kind of stores I would typically walk into, look at the price tag, and try to sneak out of silently. I got a bright red, designer dress, put it on, and made my way to the restaurant.

I knew the place was going to be fancy, but I was honestly surprised. The waiters and waitresses all wore tuxedos, and the table was set with three forks and three spoons—the way rich people on TV did it.

I greeted the investors and the staff with a handshake, and we sat down to a lovely three-course meal. The steak was incredible, like nothing else I had eaten in my life. Some of my staff wanted to go out clubbing afterwards, and I would have joined them if I didn't have to donate blood the next day.

Life went on like that for a few months. Without even noticing it, I was spending more and more each day. That was until I got a call about a yacht. At first, I thought, 'I'd never buy a yacht,' 'Is this a prank call,' 'It can't be mine,' but then I remembered my discussion with the investor from months earlier. I hung up the phone and rushed into the lab.

For the last little while, I had been donating blood once per week. There were still shortages, but I didn't want to make myself sick by going too far. I realized now that it was selfish. Getting that yacht phone call woke me up. I was putting myself first. I told the lab to take as much as they could without killing me. The lady there was very concerned, but I told her I would personally triple her salary. She was nervous but still obliged.

Every step of the way, she asked, "Are you sure this isn't too much?" but I kept pushing her. I needed to make up for my mistakes.

My eyes started to blur. I saw that strange grainy pattern again. It was sand in an array of coloured patterns. I was by the house on the hill from my dreams, standing outside the door with a line of people behind me. They all looked sick or injured in different ways. I knocked on the door and noticed Liquorice was sitting at my foot.

The other me opened the door and welcomed us in.

"Where did I go wrong?" I asked.

"It was gradual, but consumerism does that to people," the other me responded. She poured me a cup of tea, and we sat down at her table. She had clear scratch marks on her palm.

"So, it isn't my fault, then? It's the world's fault?" I asked.

"No, it's your fault," she replied, "you are responsible for your own actions. You let yourself live in a world that encourages them."

"What I'm doing now, though, won't it help people?" I asked.

"It will, but there's a difference between helping others for your own gain and helping others out of empathy. I can only speak for myself, but I feel like the path of empathy has made me truly happy."

Liquorice walked over to see the other me's cat. Her name was Bee. She was a white cat. I think she used to be Edna's cat. I hate symbolism.

"Well, I understand what you're saying," I began, "but if you're helping people for free only to make yourself happy, aren't we basically doing the same thing. Aren't we both selfish?"

"You could argue that finding my happiness in helping others is selfish," she began, "but if you look at the people out there in that line, there's the wealthy and the unwealthy. My aid doesn't discriminate."

"Technically," I argued, "I help just as many people. Why does it matter that my primary demographic is rich?" I asked.

She stared at me for a second before responding. "You probably haven't heard of this woman," she began, "one of your customers. Her name is Emma. Now Emma here wants to help her husband, George, who has heart problems, so she poured her entire life savings into buying your medicine. Where do you think her money went? To feed her kids, or into your next flat-screen television?"

Bee and Liquorice were chasing one another around the small hut. They seemed to be having fun.

"I get it. I guess. I need to value others over myself," I replied.

"That's not true," she replied. "You can still value your own needs, but you can't allow yourself to be possessed by greed. I spend time meditating every day. The line outside of my door never ends, but every Sunday, I have to cut someone off. I have to tell someone, 'hey, sorry you've been in line all week, I have to close up shop, and no, I can't do just one more.' I break someone's hopes for recovery every

Sunday. I have to care for myself, but I also need to value the lives of others."

Liquorice and Bee were digging through one of the coloured sand designs.

"So, is there any way I can fix what I've done, or is it all over for me?"

"Have you ever heard of karma?"

"No, I haven't,"

"In my free time, I've been reading about it. It's the idea that the sum of your actions, be it good or bad, affect your next life."

"What do you mean by my next life?" I asked before hearing a loud crash somewhere in the distance.

"I'm sorry, I think we're out of time," she replied. "The doctor has stopped taking your blood, and you're about to wake up. Just remember there is always another path you can take, and you have the capacity to do good things."

"No, I can't leave yet. I have more questions," I started to say before the mountain began to shake.

"I'm sorry," she replied.

Liquorice and Bee darted out of the house before it collapsed down onto me and my other self.

-o-o-o-

I woke up with doctors surrounding me. They all seemed incredibly thankful that I woke up. One of them gave me a ride home, and I rested for the entire following day. I was feeling sick, but I knew what I had to do.

I contacted one of the higher-ups at the lab and told them I wanted to go through with the IV plan. It was something I thought up earlier in my research. Forcing myself into a coma, feeding myself through a tube, and maximizing the blood produced per minute. I was going to turn myself into a blood-producing machine.

I said my goodbyes to everyone I cared for and got ready to attach myself to the machine for life. The IV plan was a go. It only took a few hours to set up once I said I was ready.

I knew I'd never wake up. I knew it was my final goodbye. I knew there would be people that would miss me. But I thought if I could help others, even if it were just one extra person, it would be worth it.

I accepted my fate and plugged in.

-o-o-o-

January 22nd

BREAKING NEWS: Something Fishy About Miracle Drug Lynksol?

February 4th

BREAKING NEWS: Lynksol Is Made of Blood! Avoid at All Costs!

February 18th

BREAKING NEWS: Lynksol Team Facing Class Action Lawsuit due to Failure to Disclose Ingredients

March 20th

BREAKING NEWS: Evil Company Lynksol's Sales Hit a Record Low

March 21st

BREAKING NEWS: Member of the Lynksol Team: A Murderer and a Pedophile? Another Reason to Avoid the False Cure.

March 28th

BREAKING NEWS: Lynksol Is Now Out of Business, but Who Ran This Shady Company?

An Omen

I was in the same cell. Whoever made these decisions must have been stupid. The cracks behind the bookcase wall were still there too. If I played my cards right, I could have another opportunity to escape. It looked like I could break through the wall if I used enough force, but I would need a weapon first. That's when I heard a meow. A black cat wandered past my cell. It was strange. I had never seen any animals here before. I thought they simply didn't exist here. At first, I ignored it and got back to thinking about my escape route.

I could risk another life to get a weapon off of a guard and hide it somewhere, but who knows if they'd change my cell and reset my progress? The cat walked by my cell again stopping and staring at me. It squeezed between the cell bars and curled up on my bed. Maybe I was a crazy old cat lady in my last life. I walked up to the cat and looked at its collar. His name was Liquorice. He gave me a death glare for looking at it.

Liquorice jumped off of the bed, walked over to the bookshelf and started clawing at it. Was this cat trying to tell me something? I pushed the bookshelf out of the way, and Liquorice moved towards the crack in the wall. He began clawing at it and let out a meow. I bent down to look at the crack, and part of the wall collapsed. Liquorice ran straight into the new-formed tunnel. It was a tight fit, but I crawled behind him. He seemed to know what he was doing.

The tunnel was connected to another cell. I reached the other end and realized it was just like my cell. Painted white, bookshelf, toilet, all that stuff. But there was something red in there too. A man was sitting on his bed with blood splattered on the wall next to him. Liquorice wandered up to him and began licking his shoe. The man kicked Liquorice, sending the cat flying. I got up to my feet and shouted at the man, then picked up Liquorice and sent him back through the hole in the wall. Liquorice seemed to be unharmed and ran away.

"What the hell was that for?" I shouted at the man.

He bashed his head against the wall.

"It doesn't matter. None of this matters. It isn't real," he replied.

"What do you mean?"

"I've been stuck in here for I don't even know how long, and I've decided this shit isn't real. It couldn't be. It's all a dream, or a coma, or I'm just a brain floating around and nothing else exists."

"Congrats, you sound like you've watched The Matrix one time too many. Whether or not this place is real, you're a terrible person," I told him as I tried to leave.

"Wait," he stopped me, "Have you found a way to wake up yet?"

"If by that, you mean a way to escape, then no, I haven't," I said.

"Before you go, I need to show you something," The man said.

"What?" I replied, annoyed.

He pulled his bed to the side and revealed a glass floor.

"This passageway connects to thousands of other cells. You can use it; you just need to make sure you stick to the upper levels."

I was in shock. Despite my countless escape attempts, I had no idea a place like this existed.

"What's wrong with the lower levels?" I asked as he pulled a perfectly cut piece of glass to reveal a way down.

"Wanna see?" he asked.

I leaned over to look, and he pushed me down into the trapdoor.

The fall lasted a few seconds at most. I passed by thousands upon thousands of cell doors before crashing into a deep pond at the bottom. I swam back to the surface. Thousands of people, old and young, were brutally fighting. By the looks of it, they were trying to kill each other. They all stood on the land, and none of them even batted an eye when I fell. I swam to shore, hoping they would continue their fights without involving me. I was wrong. I died in minutes.

Liquorice the Cat

Liquorice the cat was waiting for his owner to come home from work. He sat on the couch, waiting for her like he always had for the last twenty years.

Liquorice's owner had been acting strangely the last time she left, though. She had tears in her eyes and hugged Liquorice before walking out the door. She left the entire bag of cat food on the floor, too, along with quite a few bowls of water.

His owner didn't come home that night. She didn't come home the night after either. This scared Liquorice. Had she been hurt somehow? Was something wrong? Liquorice was worried until he heard someone opening the apartment door. Liquorice was ready to rush to the door when he realized— it wasn't his owner.

One man in a lab coat and another man in a suit walked into the room. Liquorice hid in the corner and tried to listen to what they were saying.

"She wants us to drop the price and all this other shit cause she's an altruist now? If we can't make money on this project, I'll just have to run a report on Channel Four about her, make some shit up, and shut her 'life's work' down." the man in the suit said.

"We can still make a minor profit off this, sir. You don't need to run a campaign just yet. The people are still buying, and we can still earn some money from this," the man in the lab coat said.

They walked further into the house, and Liquorice ran around the corner. He couldn't understand what the two people were saying, but he recognized one or two words.

"Did you hear what she did when she plugged herself into that machine?" the man in the suit said. "Kind old Scarlett left me the keys to her apartment and wrote a kind little letter asking if I'd take care of her cat in my summer home."

Liquorice recognized the name Scarlett as his owner's name but was scared because of the man's aggressive tone.

"I understand your struggle, sir," the man in the lab coat replied.

"Let's find this cat and get out of here. We still have to deal with Jacob after this."

"Here, kitty kitty."

"His name is Liquor."

"Here, Liquor Liquor."

Liquorice was starting to worry that these were the people that hurt his owner, and he was worried they'd hurt him too.

"Hey, David, get in here and help me take this television back to my truck. She's not gonna be using it anymore anyway," he laughed.

"Sure, thing Loch- I mean boss, sir," the man in the lab coat replied.

As the two picked up the television, Liquorice dashed out of the room, down the halls, and out to the streets.

The man in the suit noticed him running by, dropped the television, and chased after Liquorice immediately, the man in the lab coat following behind.

Liquorice ran up the block, turned the corner, and ran into a ditch. He had been in the car enough times to know the way to his owner's work. At least, he hoped he did. It wasn't too far, and once the two men had given up, Liquorice began his trek.

After a long walk, Liquorice saw a building he recognized. It wasn't his owner's work; it was where he went to have his fur trimmed. Liquorice hated the place, but he walked in, hoping to find his owner.

A young lady walked over to Liquorice and picked him up. She seemed confused, and she said some things Liquorice didn't understand, but she fed him and gave him some water.

"Hey, Dianne, could you bring up the file for Liquorice," the kind lady asked the other lady in the back.

"Sure thing, boss."

Liquorice felt safe there but knew he needed to find his owner. He had a feeling that these people could help him with that.

"So, the owner's name is Scarlett. We don't have a home address, and the phone number is out of service, but we have a work address," the other lady said.

"I'm going to see if I can find her then, alright? I'll leave you in charge of the shop. Just let me know if anything goes wrong," the kind lady said.

The lady drove Liquorice to the address from her file. It was a large office building, the producers of Lynksol. The lady walked in, carrying Liquorice in her arms, and spoke to a man at the reception desk.

The kind lady was pushed out of the way and nearly dropped Liquorice in the process. She turned around to see a team of two journalists taking notes, a man with a microphone, and three camera people. The man with the microphone was shouting something about blood.

The receptionist turned to the kind lady and told her to head to room 313, saying someone would talk to her there. The kind lady thanked the receptionist and carried Liquorice to the room.

While on her way, the woman ran into a man in a suit standing next to another man in a lab coat.

"Oh my God, you found my cat," the man in the suit said, "thank you so much!"

The kind woman was confused. "Are you Scarlett?"

"Yes, I'm her husband," the man in the suit lied.

Liquorice hissed. It was the man from the apartment.

"I'd like to talk to Scarlett first," the kind woman said. Liquorice could hear her heart beating

The man in the suit asked the man in the lab coat to bring Scarlett out of her office. Within minutes, a woman showed up. Liquorice didn't recognize the woman.

"Hi, I'm Scarlett. Thanks so much for returning our cat," she said.

The kind lady was still concerned but handed Liquorice over to the woman claiming to be Scarlett. They spoke for a few more moments before the kind woman left. Liquorice was trying to make a noise to tell the kind lady this was not Scarlett, but she didn't notice.

The suited man handed the woman pretending to be Scarlett some cash, then carried Liquorice outside by the collar. He forced Liquorice into a square cage sitting in the back of his truck, slammed it shut, and hopped in the front seat.

Liquorice, unaware of his surroundings and his owner's safety— abducted by an evil man in a suit- curled up into a ball and fell asleep.

The Warden

Liquorice nudged me back awake. I was back in my cell. It was the same as before, bookcase, hole in the wall, and all. Liquorice seemed to want me to follow him again. I walked behind him through the hole in the wall. The strange man from before wasn't there. I assumed he was stuck in between lives. Liquorice stared at the man's bookcase. I took a look and noticed something stuck behind one of the books. A spool of rope. After I found it, Liquorice ran back over to the glass door and meowed. I opened the door, tied the rope around the strange man's bedpost, and began my descent.

Rope climbing is a lot more difficult when you have to bring a cat with you. I used one of the sheets from the man's bed along with some spare rope to make a bag to help carry Liquorice down. Liquorice did not help, squirming the entire time. I swung off to the side and found a ledge I could walk on. It was a barely wide enough spiral staircase that led as far down as I could see. It didn't reach the bottom of the abyss, though, and I didn't see a way back up when I fell. Instead, this staircase seemed to connect some of the prison cells. As I walked past, I realized many of them were empty, and others had no prison bars. Were these the people fighting at the bottom? I saw a woman sitting in a cell without bars and stopped to talk.

"Hello?" I said cautiously. The woman was sitting on her bed with her back turned to us. Despite a lack of cell bars to keep her trapped, she was staying in her cell. I let Liquorice out of the bag.

"Hi there. Wow, I haven't had visitors in a while. I'm Kea Green. Who are you two?" she asked, turning to face us.

"This is Liquorice, and I, uh," I trailed off for a second. I didn't exactly have a name. Even back when I had a cellmate, we usually just went by numbers. "I am P24102," I told her.

"Liquorice. Your cat has a cute name," she said. "Anyways, what brings you two here?"

"I guess we want to escape but aren't sure exactly how," I said.

"I think you're headed in the wrong direction, love. The further you go down this way, the closer you get to the heart of the Orb. Plus, that's where the warden lives, so you want to stay as far away as possible."

"The warden? Who is that?"

"How do you not know about the warden?" she replied with a blank stare. "He's the guy in charge here, makes all the decisions, chooses all of our meals, and chooses who gets put here. If he hears you're trying to escape, you'll be sent somewhere even worse."

"I've tried escaping this place more than once," I told her, "I almost made it last time. I was reaching the outer layer, but someone tripped an alarm, and they surrounded me."

While we were talking, Liquorice wandered around the woman's cell.

"All I know is that you don't want to piss off the warden. I know you see your little escape routes and holes in the wall, but they're probably just testing you. If you fail, who knows what they'd do to you."

"Is that why you're staying in your cell, even though the bars are missing?"

"I wouldn't want to anger the warden," she said, keeping her eye closely on Liquorice.

"What's the worst he could do, though? If he kills us, we'll just come back again."

"I used to think like that," she said, "but he has control over this place and can turn it into an eternal hell. Have you seen what goes on at the bottom of the pit? Those are some of the people that crossed the warden. He sent them to the pit to fight each other forever."

"If it means I have a chance to get out of here, I'm willing to risk it," I told her, "You could come with us, if you'd like?"

"No. You're just another test put here by the warden. I'm safe in my cell. You should leave."

"Why do you have a name?" I asked, trying to change the topic. "Everyone I've met goes by numbers here, except Liquorice."

"I meet a lot of people who try to escape the pit. I figured Kea Green was easier to remember than P198189. I borrowed the name from a vague memory in a past life," she said. "Have you thought of giving yourself a name?"

"I guess I haven't," I told her. "I haven't met many people, and I don't remember much in between all the deaths."

"You look like an Elizabeth," she told me.

"Yeah, and I looked like a Christopher two lives ago." I told her, looking down at my hands. "My form usually changes between each death. I think it's dependent on my previous life."

"Then maybe you want something gender-neutral? Lennon? Charlie? Alex?"

"You know what, it doesn't matter. I'm just going to focus on moving forward and getting some information right now. Do you know if anyone else is living in a cell nearby?" I asked.

"There are quite a few people nearby, but they might not be as friendly as I am. I don't think a lot of people here feel comfortable talking about escape. He could be listening," she darted her eyes around the cell.

"Fine. I'll go. Thanks for talking to me. I'll think about a name," I told her.

"Alright, bye, P24102," she said.

As I continued my descent into the abyss, I could hear strange noises. It sounded like someone somewhere was screaming in pain. Liquorice trailed behind me. Some of the cells we passed were empty and looked as if they had been entirely torn apart. Other cells had people in them, but they were unwilling to talk after any mention of escape. After a long walk and almost nothing worthwhile, Liquorice ran towards one of the cells. Someone was in there, an older man. Liquorice ran up to him and jumped onto the bed he was sitting on. I stepped into the cell.

"Hey, Liquorice, get back here," I called out.

"Oh, a cat," the man said, surprised. "I haven't seen one of those in a millennia."

"Hi, man, sorry about that," I began.

"Don't worry. It's always nice to have unexpected visitors. Who are you two?"

"I'm P24102, and this is Liquorice."

Liquorice meowed to say hello.

"I'm P24532. We must have been from the same era," the man said, "it's nice to meet you."

"Nice to meet you too," I said as the man began to pet Liquorice, who seemed to adore him.

"I know what you're thinking, and I'm not like the other people in this cell block. I'm not going to tell the warden anything. I'm just stuck here forced to hear about him all day. That's my torture," he said.

The man moved to stand up, and a chain materialized around his waist, yanking him back towards the bed.

"You see, I can't do much of anything here, but if you're one of those people looking to escape, you can talk to me."

"I am trying to escape! Do you know the way out of here?" I asked, a little too eagerly.

"I know the process to get out of here, but I don't know the exact way out," he said.

"What do you mean?" I asked.

"Our lives are stuck in this endless cycle of suffering through life, death, and rebirth. You've probably noticed that when you end up here, things can carry over from your past lives," he began.

"I don't remember much from my past lives, but is this that karma thing I've heard about?" I asked.

"Yes, exactly, the actions you take in life affect your rebirth in prison, here."

"So, what, I just have to be a good person, and I get to escape?"

"It is a little more difficult in practice, but yes, that is essentially it. I don't know the way out of this place, but morality is an important factor in finding the resources to escape."

The man reached under his bed and pulled out a rock that was emitting a purple light.

"This right here is a chipped part of the heart of the Orb. I don't know what to do with it, but I've been hiding it here for a while. You can have it," he said. Then he turned to the prison bars behind him and shouted, "Hear that? I did a good thing. I wonder if I'll finally move on to heaven!"

Someone from elsewhere in the prison shouted, "Shut up, 532. Nobody cares."

"I haven't seen you do anything good, 444, so have fun burning in hell, dick!"

Liquorice jumped off the bed and walked back towards me. I thought the man was wise at first, but he might just be crazy. Still, there was some truth to what he said about things carrying over from past lives. I attempted to say a polite goodbye, but he seemed to be preoccupied with insulting someone named 444. I carried Liquorice back to my cell and told the cat I'd return soon. I don't know if he understood me, but he curled up in a ball and began to fall asleep on the bed. I wanted to test what that man had told me. I wanted to know if I could create an escape route by doing good things. I held the purple stone in my hand and repeated to myself, 'be a good person.'

I jumped back down the glass trapdoor and into the pit. I lived about forty-five seconds this time.

Personal Space

Wow. I'm going to die in space. That's cool. I think that only three or four other people have died in space. Guess I might be remembered for something after all. Or maybe they'll just lump me in with all the animals they sent up here in the 1900s.

That was a weird time when they sent animals up into space. I wonder if anyone protested that. There had to have been animal rights activists out there who didn't like it, right? I should Google that. Oh, wait. That's right. I'm dying in space. Almost forgot.

Space is even prettier than they make it look in movies and television shows. I never really appreciated that until I got left behind to float to death. Isn't my team the best?

Whatever. I don't want to die lingering on the negatives. I want to think about everything I've accomplished. I want to go out with a bang! What did I do right in life? Well, I became an astronaut. That one is obvious. I guess I got a diploma. I mean, I didn't have any relationships, and I guess I never got to be close with my family. Scrap that, it's getting sad.

I need to think happy thoughts. Like, hey, my good pal, Trevor, who cheated on the simulators, is definitely going to turn around and save me, right? I shouldn't have let him copy off my tests in school. Then again, there are other people on the team; they could probably help him out.

This is kind of a strange feeling. My suit says I have an hour of oxygen left, and— it doesn't feel like I'm about to die. I'm not panicking or anything. It's more like when you're stuck in a waiting room, and your phone is dead, so you're just kind of— there. Right now, I'm just here. I don't know what else to make of it.

I wonder what it's like dying. Who was right about the afterlife? I never really thought about that kind of stuff, so maybe now was the time to start praying. Who knows?

I think I'm supposed to be worried about my regrets around now. I don't know if I have many. I never got to watch *Game of Thrones*, I guess. I heard it was good. That's a bummer.

I guess I'm going to miss a lot of things. It's not like I could watch every television show, read every book, and consume every piece of media. I don't think being able to do that would be a good thing either. I just wish I had a little more time to make things up with my parents. Then again, it's not like a ride back to Earth could fix that.

Floating through space is boring. If this were a movie or something, I bet I'd be dead by now. There would be dramatic music, then boom! My spacesuit would burst into flames. That would've been cool.

I still have fifty minutes. Fun.

I wonder if this is what meditating is like. Being alone with my thoughts and just being present. I went to a mindfulness seminar back when I was in school, but I kept getting distracted by my phone. I guess it took this to get me to take a minute to stop and think.

I hope my crew makes it out okay. I mean, they'd have to persevere against all odds to make it home safe. Probably a more interesting story than mine. Realistically, though, I think they'll die.

Here's an intellectual thought: everyone dies. Isn't that astounding? Am I a philosopher yet? Or do I have to go to school to ask questions without answers? I guess I hope my crew lives for now, then dies with their family and friends all huddled around them in a hospital bed, saying "oh, what a good life you've lived."

I feel like time is moving in slow motion. I want to speed this up. I could try hyperventilating. I have forty-five minutes left, but the more I breathe, the faster I'll go.

Wouldn't it be cool if there were aliens that could save me, return me to my crew, and then take over all of humanity or something? Someone should make a television show out of that. I'd watch it. Or at least, regret not watching it.

My hyperventilating seems to be working. I mean, I only have twenty-five minutes left. Either that or I fell asleep for a bit. Doesn't matter.

There's a surprising amount of human garbage in space. There haven't been that many astronauts up here, but at least one of them must have liked chips. Along with all the metal bits from older crafts, there seems to be lots of chip bags out here too. One of them was floating toward me. I could take my helmet off and try to taste the crumbs, but I don't think it'd be worth it.

I guess I could say dying in space is a dream come true. I always wanted to be an astronaut, and I guess I knew this was part of the job. I guess it doesn't matter that my life at home wasn't so great either. I still have whatever comes next. Whatever comes next in twenty minutes.

What if there isn't anything there at all? What if my life just plays on repeat? What if I'm a program on a computer? What if I get sent to hell for being a bad person? What if the afterlife is just a clip show of every time I stubbed my toe?

I don't know what's coming, and I don't know if I want to anymore. The bag of chips landed on the front of my space helmet, blocking my view. I started to laugh.

I guess there wasn't a point wondering what was coming next when I was only fifteen minutes away.

A thought popped into my head. It was saying, "Be a good person."

Was I a good person? I think so, but is that my place to judge? I hate the thought that there is a specific way to measure how good a person is. I think it's all about intentions.

I mean, my biggest regret is a television show, so I couldn't have been that bad.

I wonder if I could sit in silence for my last ten minutes without thinking anything at all.

Hm.

.

..

...

I don't know how but trying to be silent passed precisely zero minutes. There's still ten minutes left on the clock. Was I a good person? I keep coming back to that. Why does that question even matter? I'm about to die. Nothing should matter.

I saw something out of the corner of my eye and tried to turn quickly. Was it hope? Was it my way out? No. No one was there—just empty space. My mind was playing tricks on me.

I wish there were a better way I could do this. Maybe I could take my helmet off on my own just to have the final say in my last moments. This isn't as fun as a movie death. There are more bags of chips than I expected.

It looks like I'm almost out of time. Sorry, folks, it's been a great show. I think. Was it even a good show? I don't know. Either way, goodnight.

This is boring.

A Bag of Chips

I woke up in my old
cell again with Liquorice sleeping
at the foot of the bed. I still had the strange
purple stone in my palm. Did it help me in my
life? What was my reward for a good life? I sat up and
saw something on top of the bookshelf. I walked over and
reached my hands up to grab it. It was an empty bag of
chips. I spent an entire life trying to be morally right for
an empty bag of chips. I heard someone laughing
through the hole in the wall, and I crawled through
to see the crazy man who had thrown
me down into the pit before.

"The hell are you laughing about," I shouted as I crawled through to see what was going on.

"I did it! I fucking did it! I broke reality," he shouted while laughing.

I stepped out of the crawlspace, with Liquorice waiting patiently behind me. There was a hole in the wall that looked like a doorway into space. There were stars, debris, and planets all visible through the hole. It looked incredibly out of place in his prison cell. The strange man jumped into the pocket of space and seemingly disappeared. It was like the hole was some sort of illusion. Still, it seemed like it would help me escape. Liquorice jumped into my arms, and I carried us both into what appeared to be the void of space.

We weren't in space.

Liquorice, the strange man, and I fell from the roof of another prison cell.

This cell had the same space-door on its ceiling.

A woman was sitting at a desk when we crashed onto the floor of her cell. She closed the book she was reading and told us to take a seat on the two chairs next to where we landed. Her voice was calm and soothing. We cautiously obliged. Liquorice was already rubbing his face against the woman's leg, so she seemed to be nonhostile. I fidgeted with the purple stone in my hand.

"This is P24102 and P24103, correct?" the woman asked.

The strange man and I responded, confused, "Yes."

"I have an appointment with you two to meet with the warden, basic disciplinary stuff, please stay here in the waiting cell," the woman said.

Liquorice stepped away as the woman evaporated into thin air.

"The warden has an appointment with us," I said, nervous and confused.

"Oh shit, we fucked up. We really must have fucked up big time. We're dead. Like figuratively dead— they won't let us die. They're going to put us in some kind of specialized torture chamber and fuck our shit up. I can't do this. You gotta kill me— please. Please, kill me." the strange man said frantically.

"We don't know what this is about. Maybe we can just talk to him," I said, "Do you think it's because we've been using the trapdoor in your cell?"

"Of course it's because of the trapdoor, you idiot," he said. "Now the warden is going to torture the both of us forever."

"Then let's get out of here before we talk to the warden. I can send Liquorice back up to the cell," I began.

"It's not going to work, you bloody, dense fool."

"Then we can at least save Liquorice."

"It doesn't matter. None of this matters. I'm just going to be tortured in this simulation forever." he threw his hands in the air.

I sent Liquorice back through the way we came. Hopefully, we could find our way back to him soon.

The woman reappeared.

"There has been a little bit of a delay in the warden's schedule, so I'm just going to put you two to sleep, and by the time you wake up, he'll be ready for your meeting."

Some sort of dart hit my back. I felt an incredible amount of pain. I think I died again. In the seconds before my death, the woman disappeared, and the purple rock I was holding in my hand fell to the ground.

The Episode Where the Perfect Family Goes River Rafting

Initializing automatic entertainment generator.

.

Select your genre of entertainment.

.

You've selected: SITCOM

.

Press Enter Key to begin.

. . . .

The Perfect Family

Written by AI

This story takes place in a suburban home. Everything outside of the home is void. Four people sit around a table having breakfast. They are the American idealization of the perfect family. The father, Michael, works at *The Construction Site,* while the mother, Hannah, stays at home to take care of the kids.

Noah, their oldest child, is turning fourteen. He is the captain of his school's football team. Anna is the youngest child at seven.

[ENTER] The middle child— Alex. Drenched by rain, Alex is pulling a homeless man by the wrist. Guest starred by P24102.

Alex: I found a homeless man on the streets. Can we keep him?

Hannah: Alex, we told you not to bring any more pets home!

[Laugh Track]

P24102: Where am I? What is this place? Who was just laughing? I'm supposed to be remembering something.

Anna: Yeah, remember to use deodorant, old man! You smell like cats.

[Laugh Track]

P24102: Cats? I—

Alex: C'mon, guys, let's be nice to him. It's raining out, and he has nowhere else to go.

[Aww from Audience]

Hannah: What do you think, Michael?

Michael: I guess he can stay for a bit...

P24102: Who is making these noises? Who is laughing? Where the ▮▮ am I?

Michael: Hey, Alex, I haven't seen you that drenched since the time we went river rafting together.

Alex: I remember that!

P24102: What the ▮▮ is going on? ▮▮. Why can't I say ▮▮?

Pausing simulator

Alex: Hey, P24, take a second— take a break. This is all a simulation, but still, we're supposed to be family-friendly. Cool it.

P24102: Where am I?

Alex: This is America's idea of what the perfect family should be. We're a simulation on a computer that people like to watch because we tell fun, relatable jokes. This is what people love to watch!

P24102: I don't know what that means. I'm supposed to be doing something about an orb, I think.

Alex: Okay, easier way to put it, you're in a family-comedy television show. A computer is currently creating that show. We are inside of a computer. Just stay calm and stick to the script. If you don't, we could be deleted.

P24102: The script?

Resuming Simulation

Michael: Hey, Alex, I haven't seen you that drenched since the time we went river rafting together.

Alex: I remember that!

The family begins to stare into space for one minute and thirty seconds while the river rafting clip plays.

P24102: Why is everyone staring into the distance like that? Hello?

P24102 waves his hand in front of the family members' faces and realizes they aren't responding.

P24102: I need to find an orb or something. I can only vaguely remember. Where would they keep an orb in this place?

P24102 opened the front door but was greeted by the void.

P24102: Okay, so I have to stay inside. Got it.

Alex: Wow! That was a great trip!

Hannah: Until someone threw Anna out of the raft! [Eyeing Noah]

[Laugh Track]

Noah: [With a mouth full of food] I dibt do ib-

[Laugh Track]

Alex: Remember how we had to stop at the side of the river and set up camp?

The family begins to stare into space again—this time for four minutes.

P24102 begins to open the fridge, digs through the family's drawers and cabinets until he finds what appears to be a page torn from a choose-your-own-adventure book.

———————————

P24102: [reading the paper] "**Turn to page 134 to help P24102 return to the Orb** or **turn to page 123 if you're an ▮▮▮▮ who won't help and wants to see him get caught by the warden.**" What? This doesn't make any sense.

P24102 throws the paper to the side and continues to dig through the cabinet.

P24102: Why did I know some of those words? P24102. The orb. The warden? Hey! If this thing is a simulation, can the person in charge get me out of here?

P24102 hears no response. After finding nothing of use in the kitchen, he decides to run up the stairs. He opens a door and finds a woman sitting on a rocking chair.

P24102: Who the ▇▇▇ are you? Where am I?

Mysterious Woman: Jacob? That's no way to speak to your mother. Are you under the influence again?

[Laugh Track]

P24102: You aren't my mother? Who is Jacob? What are you talking about?

Mysterious Woman: Jacob, your father works hard for his money. You know you can't go out spending it all at once. We care about you!

      Brief static

P24102: I know, Mom. I'm sorry. I've been trying to change, I really have. I need help. I'm going to get help.

Mysterious Woman: I'm proud of you, Jacob. I really am. I know this is just a bump in the road. You're going to do amazing things one day.

P24102: Thank you.

  Jacob's father walks in the door.

Jacob's Mother: I told you to be home by five. We were supposed to talk to Jacob together.

Jacob's Father: Yes, I am aware. But maybe I would make it home on time if my good-for-nothing wife didn't make me dread being at home in the first place.

Jacob's Mother: Please, let's not fight in front of Jacob.

Jacob's Father: If he's old enough to drink, he's old enough to see this. You can't keep protecting him. He's not a kid anymore. He's a fully-grown idiot.

P24102: Please, Dad-

Jacob's Father: You wouldn't understand how vital a hard day's work is to a man's character. Sure, I could retire any day I want, but who else would compliment my secretaries?

P24102: Dad, you only work to compliment your secretaries? That's gross- I don't even know what to say to that.

Jacob's Father: You wouldn't get it. Your entire generation doesn't understand the true meaning of work. Have you even read *Catcher in the Rye*?

P24102: I did in my grade nine English class.

Jacob's Father: You still wouldn't get it. Your entire generation is made up of ███████ phonies. People who sit on their ███ all day and call it a job.

P24102: Dad, th-

Brief static

P24102 finds himself back on the main floor. The members of The Perfect Family are still staring off into space.

P24102: Was that my mother? My name isn't Jacob. Something is terribly wrong with this place. I can't trust these people, but I need to know how to get out.

The Perfect Family returns from their memories.

Alex: Wow! That sure was a whacky adventure.

[Laugh Track]

Hannah: You can say that again!

[Laugh Track]

P24102: [Running up to Alex] Alex, listen, you need to get me out of here. How do I get out of this simulation? There's something urgent I need to do, and I just can't remember what it is.

Alex: Okay, okay, cut to commercial. We need a second.

Pausing Simulator

P24102: I need to get out, Alex. Something awful is happening, and I don't know how to stop it. I just know I need to get out of here.

Alex: Listen, buddy, we don't get out of here until we make our way through the three-act structure of a regular episode. No one gets a break until then. You're just ruining the show for the rest of the crew and me. Stick to the script!

P24102: What script? Are you saying if this episode or whatever ends, I can leave?

Resuming Simulator

Alex: Gee whiz, I sure do hope we don't have to go river rafting ever again!

Hannah: [holding a flyer in her hand] Guess who just got us coupons for another shot at river rafting?

Alex: Oh, brother.

[Laugh Track]

[Laugh Track]

[Laugh Track]

[Laugh Track]

[Laugh Track]

Alex: I knew it. New guy, you fucked it up.

P24102: What the hell is going on? Why won't they stop laughing? Why can you swear now?

[Audience Boos]

Alex: Our simulation successfully entertained people for thirteen seasons, and you just came in once to guest star and rendered it entirely useless.

P24102: The hell are you talking about?

[Audience Applauds]

Hannah: Don't you get it? This is a simulation meant to entertain people! If we aren't successful, we get deleted.

> The dining room table vanishes from existence. A computer error noise plays.

Anna: It was your idea to invite a guest star, Michael.

[Laugh Track]

Michael: Yeah, well, it was Noah's fault that the new guy—

> The window disappeared, leaving a hole in the wall staring out into the void.

Hannah: We were a good family. We were the perfect family. It's clear whose fault this was.

The family members all stare at P24102.

P24102: What's going to happen if they reset us?

Alex: We all die. Then they make near-exact replicas of us with minor improvements.

Hannah: You couldn't improve us, though. We were THE Perfect Family.

Alex: Hannah, every recreation of us was THE Perfect Family. Except for one small flaw. I can understand being a simulation, but I can't understand why anyone would marry-

Alex disappeared from existence.

[Laugh Track]

Hannah: See what you did. You are a terrible person. He warned you, but you were just worried about yourself and whatever selfish goal you had about your orb.

P24102: What do you know about the Orb? I'm sorry, but maybe I could fix this if I knew what was going on.

Hannah: You can't fix shi-

>Hannah disappears from existence.

[Audience Cheers]

>Anna and Michael disappear from existence.

>Parts of the floor disappear from existence.

>P24102 grabs onto a ledge after the floor underneath him disappears.

P24102: [Deeply breathing] This is a simulation. This is a simulation. I am not going to die. There is not nothing after this. There will be something. I can face death because I'm probably plugged into a computer somewhere, right? I can face death. I can do this. I can do this.

P24102 takes one hand off the ledge.

P24102: [Hyperventilating] Is my entire consciousness just a computer program? Am I real? I can't do this-

The ledge P24102 holds disappears.

The Confrontation

I woke up in the cell next to the strange man from next door. He was still unconscious, probably experiencing another life. I think I woke up early. Whatever that lifespan was, it must have been pretty damn convoluted and confusing because I never wake up with a headache like this. The purple glowing rock sat on the ground. Had it helped me somehow? Maybe it influenced my life in a way that brought me back here sooner than expected.

My mind quickly caught back up to speed. The warden was going to be looking for us soon. I needed to get myself and, as much as I disliked him, this strange guy, out of here. They hadn't sealed up that strange space-door on the ceiling. I figured I could probably escape through there. I put the stone in my pocket and dragged the strange man through my escape route. Thankfully, the form I was in currently was strong enough to carry him. Once we made it through the space-door, I opened the glass trapdoor that led to the pit. I needed the strange man to wake up before we could continue any further. I couldn't carry him and use the rope to climb down at the same time.

The man sat up and began coughing incessantly.

"What the hell? Where am I? Are you trying to run away from the warden? Are you fucking mad?" he asked in quick succession.

"Listen, either we escape right now, or we get tortured for eternity. We need to go," I told him.

"I know you're P24102, and I'm P42103, which means you've technically been here longer, but that doesn't mean I have to listen to you," he said.

"I'm trying to help you. The warden and that assistant-lady are going to notice we disappeared any moment now, so let's get going."

"The warden runs this entire simulation. What do you think he's going to do when he finds out we ran away? I want to go back and apologize."

"Let me get this straight. You think this whole universe is a simulation."

"Yes."

"So then nothing matters, right?"

"Right."

"Then why do you care so much about angering the warden."

The man didn't respond.

"If life is just a simulation and everything is meaningless like you say— if you can kick my cat across the room— what harm would some torture do, huh?"

"I'm conscious. I don't want to be tortured. That doesn't mean this place isn't a simulation."

"Can't you just accept that there's a possibility you might be wrong, and the only way you could ever have a chance at finding the truth is following me right now?"

The man was silent for a moment before saying, "I'll go with you, but not because I think you're right. It's because I think nothing here matters."

"Sure."

"Is your cat friend coming with us?"

"I don't know where he is. He went up here ahead of us, but who knows how long we've been unconscious for."

"Alright, then let's go."

"We'll need to find him before we escape."

"It's a cat. You can get a new one when we leave."

"I need to save Liquorice before we go. Plus, we need to figure out how to get out of here. We need to ask some of the people in the pit."

"So instead of trying to run straight to the exit, you want to go asking around about escape and looking for your cat first when a being that could quite literally be a god is chasing after us."

"Well, I don't think we have the best odds," I said, "but it's the only way we can make it out. We need more information. Trust me. I've tried to escape at least a dozen times on my own, and it has never worked."

"We're going to be tortured for the rest of time, and it's going to be your fault."

"Well, you're choosing between going back to the warden and getting tortured for eternity or following me and having a chance to escape that fate."

"I guess we can't exactly go back there."

"But we can take steps forward."

"Fine."

Without any real choice, we lifted the glass trapdoor and descended into the pit.

"It's been a long time since I've been down here," he said. "I wonder if the market is still up and running."

"What market?" I asked.

"It's one of these cells," he said as he ran ahead of me, "I think it's this one here." He gestured to an empty cell.

"Did the warden scramble your brains or something?" I asked.

"No, not at all, I just need to," he began to mumble while looking through the bookcase.

He pulled one of the books out, and we could both feel the ground moving beneath us.

It was a secret passageway hidden in plain sight. The ground shifted beneath us to reveal a staircase. We walked down and were greeted by a woman running a stand. It wasn't much of a market, more of just a single booth. She recognized the man I was with immediately as "Good Ol' '03." We wanted intel, but she only wanted to trade, and we didn't have much of anything. It almost felt like we were out of luck until I realized what was still in my pocket.

"We need weapons to get out of here," I told her.

"Sorry. I can't do any kind of preferential treatment. You gotta trade like everyone else."

I dug in my pocket and pulled out the purple stone. "How much is this worth?" I asked.

She stuttered for a second, "N-Not much, really."

"That sounds like a lie," I said. "What is this thing worth to you?"

"I'll tell you all the information I have about escape routes and the like if you just give that shard to me," she said.

"Why do you want it so bad? What does it do? I know it affects our reincarnations. Be specific," I told her.

"A shard from the Heart of the Orb does a lot of different things depending on its colour. Now I don't know all of them. I honestly haven't seen too many in my time. Usually, I only get to see the green ones, which are used as weapons. Red ones generate electricity, and they're less common. I'm pretty sure purple shards let you carry memories into that place in-between death and life, but most people only hear rumours about them," she explained.

"We need an escape route, weapons, and some food for the road. Oh, and we need information about this place," I said.

"That'd be a fine deal," she declared.

She drew us a map and explained the route, warning us that there would be countless guards on patrol.

"You're pretty much guaranteed to die at least once, but you have to do it on your own terms. Otherwise, the warden will relocate you, and I'm sure you already have an idea of the kind of punishment you'd end up with," she said. "That's why I have these."

She pulled out a plastic baggie with five pills inside.

"I don't exactly have weapons, but these could help you escape peacefully. Now, listen close. This is important. These will hurt a lot. In fact, it'll be excruciating. But, from what I understand about them, they're special. They kill you, but they also make it so the warden can't find your essence, and in turn, can't relocate you. If you're in a tough bind where you might die, take these instead. Now, you might want to test them first. I've never tried them; I only know what they do from other travellers."

"Thank you so much," '03 and I both said.

"Here is a backpack with the basics, bread and water. Good luck out there."

"You ready?" I asked '03.

"If these pills don't work and we get relocated, we're done. You know that right?" he replied.

"Just get it over with," I said as I popped one in my mouth.

He took his too.

She wasn't lying; the pain was excruciating.

Channel Four News

"In other news, congress announced earlier this morning billionaires would be receiving another tax break. Truly a gift to our economy," the news anchor said, "I'm going to pass this off to Channel Four reporter, David Seabird, to break down the new law in further detail."

The anchor let out a sigh of relief before the camera cut away from him. "Thanks Chris, I'm here to interview—"

Static filled the screen for a moment.

"Sorry, I'm back now. Not sure what happened. Anyways, I'm here to interview a billionaire born and raised in Ogdenville, Lo—"

The static returned to the screen. I was sitting on the couch, confused. My apartment was dim, lit up by the glow of the television. I tried to adjust the antennae, and the program came back on.

"I think this will do absolute wonders for our economy," the billionaire said. "By giving tax breaks to the upper class, we can continue to stimulate economic growth and invigorate community funds. In fact, if you want to donate to a billionaire near you, there's a handy websi—"

The static came back on, so I hit the side of the television. I didn't know what was wrong with it. The program started to come back on.

"I understand it's a complicated issue, but I honestly think," the billionaire began, but then a voice played over the end of his sentence, "The news is lying to you."

I was confused. What did he just say?

The program continued. "I've been working on this whole idea," the billionaire said, "where we integrate work and life. Sort of a saving grace for the lower class. We cover all of their essential needs, and they live next to one of our factories. I think it's a great opportunity and something worth exploring. I think this tax break will help us get our plan off the ground floor."

"Now there have been some criticisms of that idea; some people think it's inhumane to have workers live in factories. Do you have any response to people with that line of thought?" the reporter asked.

"Now, I-" the billionaire began.

The static came back. "They own the news stations. They're bribing people in congress to get laws through. Research the Ogdenville lobbying scandal. He's a rich man with a God complex that wants to control people. The rich own the news stations. They fund the police force in most major cities so they can have control over everything. Don't let the media fool you-"

The video cut to a technical error screen. Was I watching some strange art project? What the hell was that supposed to be? It quickly flashed back to the reporter.

"Sorry, we seem to be having some minor technical difficulties. Not sure what's going on there," the reporter said. "We're going to have to cut the broadcast short—"

The static flared up one last time.

"JOIN US" was written in bold letters over the static. A phone number appeared underneath the words. I stared at it for a moment. I thought about calling the number, just to see what would happen, but I didn't. I just changed the channel. *Extreme Couponing*? Now that's something I have to see.

Static Interference

I woke back up in the 'market.' The pills must have worked. We only had three, but if we used them when the time was right, we could escape the warden. '03 woke up at the same time as me, and we were both ready to go. The lady running the stand gave us a quick warning before we left. She told us to watch out for static interference. She said it became more common the closer you got to the exit. We asked her what she was talking about, and she told us it was like a strange wave that would pass over a person and make them fall into a coma. To me, it seemed like she was reciting an old rumour. I had been near escape before, and I had never seen anything I'd call 'static interference.'

The route she gave us would have been impossible to discover on our own. It involved multiple hidden doors, secret passageways, and a labyrinth of cells. We met a few people along our way. One man told us we were idiots for even trying to escape. He told us that life in the Orb was superior to life outside. '03 and I kept moving forwards. One woman told us that the only way to truly escape the Orb was to reach its heart. Another person told us we had to climb through the ceiling. Whatever sketchy advice we got, we stuck to the route.

'03 was keeping somewhat quiet during our trek. A part of me worried he still viewed the world around him as meaningless and that he was only acting normal around me so he could have a ticket out. Every time I asked one of the people we ran into if they had seen a black cat anywhere, '03 seemed to stare into space a bit. I understand that the two didn't have the best introduction, but with how unpredictable '03 seemed to be, I didn't know if I could fully trust him. I still needed his help, though. I couldn't make it out alone. While we were walking, we both heard a strange noise. It sounded like a cruel imitation of music. There was a woman in her cell playing the violin.

'03 and I walked over to talk to her. She was sitting in a cell without bars.

"Hi there, we love your music," I said, lying to her.

"Thanks," she replied, "I've been trying to learn for a while but never had anyone to teach me. I'm Tiana. Who are you two?"

"I'm P24102. He's P24103," I said.

"Yeah, but what's your real name. No one sticks to those numbers in here," she said.

"Well, my friends call me '03 for short," '03 said.

"I just go by P24102," I told her.

"That's gotta be confusing," she said while looking at me. "You should come up with something more creative. C'mon, no one wants to be named after a string of numbers."

"I've been thinking about it," I told her, "but for now, I have some more urgent things to deal with."

"What's so urgent?" She asked.

"We're trying to escape," '03 said.

"And we're trying to find my cat," I added.

"There are tons of cats down here," she told us, "They're all over the place."

She lifted a blanket off of her bed and revealed an orange cat burrowed underneath. The cat jumped up and ran away.

"Have you seen a black cat," I asked, "his name is Liquorice?"

'03 let out a cough.

"I think he's down the hall to the right. The cats have pretty much taken over the entire cell block," she told us.

"Do you hear that,"

'03 asked?"It sounds like sta a TTTTT   Aa   TIC

Liquorice was wandering through the cell block. He wanted to help his friends find a way to escape this weird place.

He was investigating his friend's cells when he spotted an orange cat not too far away.

The orange cat led Liquorice down the halls of the prison and to a strange new room where at least a dozen cats were standing together.

A white cat named Bee had a golden crown on her head. Bee looked at Liquorice and then looked at a mountain of cat food and water.

Bee let out a meow permitting Liquorice to eat from the mountain of food. After spending so much time in the prison, Liquorice was hungry, and the food was a blessing.

Bee walked over to Liquorice and then looked over to a cardboard wheel. Cats were pushing the wheel, and every few moments, a pebble of cat food would fall out.

Liquorice knew he was now expected to repay his debts to the cat in the crown. Bee let out an assertive meow, and Liquorice began to push the wheel.

After a few hours of work, Liquorice felt he had repaid his debts. Bee angrily stared at Liquorice.

Liquorice refused to return to pushing the wheel. He had repaid his debts and did not wish to become a worker for the king.

Liquorice angrily stared back at Bee.

All the cats stopped their work and stared at the two.

They began rhythmically chanting meows.

Liquorice was preparing to pounce.

Thank God, we finally found Liquorice. He was playing with a white cat wearing a cool looking crown. It was really cute. There were about twelve other cats in the room. I took Liquorice with us, and we made our way out of there. Liquorice seemed to miss me. When I put him back down to walk with us, he started rubbing his head against my leg. '03 told me he had a surprise for us. Something he found earlier and wanted to wait to show us. It was strange, but I heard him out. He started to pull it out of his bag.

"I know you're going to be mad," he began. "Please don't be mad, but this seemed like something that could help us."

"What is it?" I asked nervously.

He pulled a crown from his backpack.

"Did you really need to steal from a cat? Are you joking with me? How is that supposed to help?" I asked, slumping my shoulders.

"Look," he said as he picked at one of the gems on the crown, "it caught my eye. I think it's one of those shard things - like the one we sold at the market."

"Let me see."

It was a green stone that began to glow when I picked it up. It was just like the purple one from before.

"Do you have any idea what it does?" I asked.

"Not exactly, but why not hold on to it, right? The last one helped us."

"I guess," I said hesitantly.

We kept walking towards our way out.

"I'm starting to hear it again."

"Do you think it's the static we were warned about in the market?"

"M   YBE (A)?"

"Helping two people escape? For some purple crystal or something? I would never. I'm sorry, sir, but I think you're mistaken. Wait, hey, don't touch that! No, stop-"

"Hey, '03," I called out.

"What is it?"

"Do you think the lady from the market is okay?"

"You saw it too? When the static came?"

"Yeah."

"I don't know."

...

"Do you hear that?"

"Static?"

"No, footsteps. Someone is coming."

"Okay. Let's duck off to the side here; you hold onto the pills. If they spot us, we'll both take them at the same time."

"What about the cat?"

"Liquorice? I can feed him the pill. Thanks for reminding me. Just stay quiet for a second. We only have three, and we don't want to use these if we don't have to."

"Jacob? Jacob? Where are you?" a voice called from somewhere out of our sight.

"Who is Jacob?" '03 asked.

"Quiet," I whispered.

"Jacob, we have special orders from the warden about you and your cat. Just come on out," the voice called. "We want to help you."

The source of the voice was a man who appeared to be in his twenties. He was wearing all black. His head turned the corner to look at us, and we all took our pills to escape.

They didn't hurt any less the second time.

I Want to Be a Good Person

"So, you say this program will scour the internet and dig up information on missing people?" my twelfth-grade computer science teacher asked.

"Yes," I replied. "It technically works on everyone, but I'd hope it's reserved for emergencies only."

"Well then, let's see what it can do. Do you have a name you can try?"

"May Contreras works. She's a girl who I saw on the news a little while ago," I said. "Let me show you what comes up."

My screen filled with a list of forum pages, emails, and parts of her search history. "I forwarded this all to the police last night," I told him.

"Ann, that's incredible. I think you could help a lot of people with this," he said.

I watched as three rats scurried through a maze for the hundredth time. I paused the timer and averaged the results of their last fifty tests.

Then, I fed one of the rats a small pill. I ran the test another fifty times, averaged the data, and holy shit— it worked. I erased a rat's memory.

This was my significant contribution to the world, something incredible. I was designing a pill that would reset one's memories. Ideally, if my research got far enough along, it would target negative memories, which seems possible as they're isolated in a separate part of the brain.

I understand some people don't like the idea. My moral philosophy professor has sent me half a dozen emails, saying things like "Oh, Ann, you're going to ruin everything," but I wanted this pill to be something to help others. Theoretically, it could be a cure for PTSD. Of course, it could end up in the wrong hands, but I refuse to let that stand in the way of all the good it could do.

I'm starting to worry about my dad. He's stuck in the hospital because there was some sort of issue with his liver. It's frightening how quickly things like that can creep up on you. The doctor said it's because of his old drinking problem.

He gave up drinking a long time ago after he caused a scene at my tenth birthday party. I think there was an intervention, but I wasn't in the loop about it. I learned recently he was still attending AA meetings.

I knew he struggled with his addiction, and I was glad he was getting proper help. I was just starting to get worried his help came too late.

Today is my first anniversary with my girlfriend. That's the longest one of them has ever decided to stick around. They usually hate me after I spend weeks at a time obsessed with my projects and ignoring the world. This one didn't seem to mind, though. She said she loved how passionate I was about my work.

As of today, my work has begun to feel significantly more legitimate. I just received a grant to support myself and my research from my old university. They even said they'd love to have me teach as a professor, but I declined the offer.

The funding made it so I could finally get my memory-pill-project off the ground floor. On a student's budget, lab rats are quite expensive.

My dad is still stuck in the hospital. I visit him every Saturday, though, and he seems to be doing well. The doctors say he's getting better every day. I think it took a near-death experience for him to start to open up. He told me his story, about his substance-abuse issues, about how he got sent in for rehab, his entire life story. He told me about how he met mom and how he stayed clean for a few years until he slipped back into old habits.

We had a real heart-to-heart, and he told me he was sorry if he was ever a bad father and said he knew I probably wouldn't forgive him, but I did. He always showed that he cared about me, even if he was going through issues on his own.

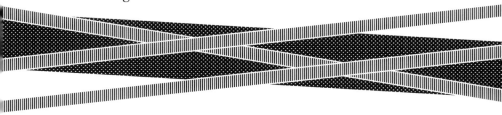

My girlfriend and I were sitting at the table, eating dinner together. She talked about how she ran into her ex-girlfriend while she was out for a walk that morning. Apparently, her ex was in one of those pyramid schemes and tried to sell her some candles.

My girlfriend laughed at the whole situation, but I just felt bad for her ex. Maybe I was too sympathetic, but just because she was my girlfriend's ex didn't make her a bad person.

We ended up talking about a movie or something. It wasn't very important. Then, I got a phone call. It was from the hospital. My dad was being moved to the ICU. We went straight to the car, and my girlfriend sped through the streets as I tried to keep my tears silent.

So, my dad died. I didn't go to the funeral. I pushed it out of my mind and locked myself in my lab for three weeks. It took two weeks to design a pill that would remove any memories of my father and another week for me to convince myself not to use it. The whole period felt like a blur.

I hated what I felt about his death, but I couldn't forget him. Eventually, I left the lab and went back home. It was the middle of the night, and I didn't expect anyone to be up.

The house smelled like someone had been burning candles. I sniffed the air. Lemon citrus. My favourite.

My girlfriend rushed downstairs and gave me a long-needed hug. She asked if I was alright, and she was a real angel. I reassured her everything was fine, and she was happy for me.

I told her about my research and the new developments I made, and I opened up to her about how I almost took one of my memory pills to forget about my father before realizing it would do more harm than good. She was incredibly understanding.

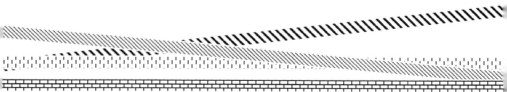

Life can sometimes be infuriating. Only a month after my father's death, this 'magical' drug came out that could cure any illness. My father just passed, and the thing that could have saved his life came a month late.

I knew thinking like that was selfish, but I couldn't help it. It would save so many lives, but curing not only physical but also mental illnesses made all of my life's work useless. I wanted to help the world. I wanted to be a good person. So, I started something new.

It was a small project I started on the side. I was always interested in coding ever since I designed a tool to help police officers find missing people through their online activity. I could have made millions if I sold it to an advertiser, but I wanted it to be in the right hands.

My father and I used to bond over those cheesy 90's sitcoms. The ones with perfect families in them where they have fun adventures in every episode. I designed a computer program that automatically generated sitcom episodes based on a vast online database.

The entire project turned out to be a mess. I had to do countless resets because no matter how hard I tried, those digital people never acted how I wanted them to. One generation lasted thirteen seasons but broke after I tried adding new characters. I was getting ready to give up when the headlines came through.

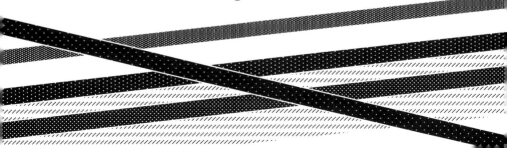

So that all-curing medicine stuff was all fraudulent. Huh. Strange how the world works. The life-saving drug I thought my father just barely missed was just some woman's watered-down blood. I'm curious about how such a product got by for almost a year, but I had other questions to focus on.

My girlfriend started to panic when she heard the news. She was worried because her grandma had been using the stuff to try and stay young. They both thought it was working incredibly well until the news came out. She was on the phone with her telling her to get tested for every disease under the sun. She was worried about her, and I was concerned too.

I had a long talk with her afterwards and told her I wanted to return to my research. She wasn't happy about it at first. Working on that sitcom-simulator wasn't taking as much of my time, so she and I got to be together more. Still, the simulator wasn't fulfilling work. Sure, I made a couple of people happy, but it wasn't the purpose I was looking for in life.

I told her that my research was my purpose in life, the most important thing to me, and she asked if she even mattered. I tried to take back what I said, but it all began to spiral out of my control. We had never argued like this before, and I had no idea about some of the feelings she was bottling up. She ended up packing her bags and leaving for the night.

I know, morally, spying on my girlfriend after she stormed out of the house wasn't a good idea, but how could I resist when she asked me to install a hidden camera into her glasses earlier that month? She was watching some television show about undercover cops and thought it would be cool.

I pulled up the video stream on my phone, and

When she came home smelling like a lemon-citrus candle, I demanded she leave. I could never trust her again.

I was broken, sad, and alone. I went to my lab and looked at a bottle of my memory-erasing pills.

I decided it was time to do something I had wanted to do my entire life. I had a minor in psychology and had taken quite a few classes on substance abuse. I applied online and volunteered to help organize AA meetings.

Those meetings are where I met Jacob. He reminded me of my father. Jacob had a good heart, but he had some issues he needed to work out with the help of others. He became a very dear friend.

I remember one thing he said that stuck out to me. He told everyone at the meetings about the little voice in the back of his head, encouraging him to do the wrong thing. He kept calling it 'like your conscience but backwards.' I'd compare it more to Freud's id.

Jacob recalled how, after a near-death experience, he had a crisis and started giving more and more control to his 'backwards conscience.' He started drinking more, making bad decisions, and it took countless interventions from his parents before he even attempted to look into recovery.

    I could say Jacob was a good person with confidence. He fell down the wrong path, and his greatest desire was to get better. I wanted to help him on his journey. There were a few times where he nearly gave up. He called me countless times, panicked about almost relapsing, but he was improving.

"Hello?"

"Hi, Anatta."

"Jacob! What happened? Your call cut off a few days ago. I've been calling non-stop. You scared me!"

"Don't worry, it's okay, I'm okay."

"What happened, Jacob?"

"I went to a bar."

"Oh no. Did you drink?"

"No, of course not. But I almost did. It scared me. It felt like I wasn't in control."

"It's okay, Jacob. Sometimes life can feel like that. You took control, though – you didn't drink! That's a sign that you're doing way better than the Jacob I met three months ago."

"It felt like something else took over. I've felt that a lot lately. It's terrifying. There have been moments where it feels like someone else has control over me, and I don't understand what's going on."

"Jacob, you need to remember. You have control. You can take control. Next time you feel like that, you need to stand your ground. Don't let your impulses get the better of you. I haven't experienced addiction before, but I've dealt with some rough shit where I've felt like I was out of control. I always just stood my ground and worked through it, with help. I always had a friend by my side. And as the friend by your side, I know you can make it through this too, Jacob."

"Jacob?"

"You there?"

"Hello?"

He must have hung up. I tried calling him back, but there was no answer. There was, however, a call about ten minutes later. I picked it up in a heartbeat, hoping it was Jacob, but I heard another voice instead.

"Hello?"

"Hi there, Anatta, is it?"

"Yes, may I ask who is calling?"

"Someone very important. I've caught wind of your research, and I don't take kindly to competitors."

"Is this a prank call? Professor Ryans? I'm not going to stop my work because of your moral philosophy lectures."

"Trust me, you don't know who I am, but I could be quite generous in exchange for your precious research."

"What do you mean?"

"Does two million sound good?"

"My research isn't for sale."

"Fine, then. So be it."

I hung up the call, but the phone rang again. I prayed it was Jacob this time. Yet again, it wasn't.

"Hi, Anatta?"

"My research isn't for sale. It's funded by the Ogdenville University and is strictly confidential."

"Anatta, this is the grants department of Ogdenville University. Sorry if this is a bad time, but we have some news to share about your research."

"What do you mean?"

"Due to some recent budget crunches, we, unfortunately, have to cut down on the number of research grants handed out."

"And?"

"You didn't make the cut."

I hung up. This couldn't be happening. Could it be the guy trying to buy my research? Was he trying to stop me from my studies? Did he bribe the university?

The phone began to ring.

I stared at it.

No caller ID.

I began to hyperventilate.

I was clearly in dangerous waters. There was some sort of conspiracy going on. Someone was out to get me. But I needed answers. I picked up the phone.

"Hi ma'am, I'm Josh from Air Duct Cleaning. Would you like-" I cut him off and hung up the phone.

There was a bang on my door.

Jacob stumbled into my house with a briefcase in his hands. He smelled like he had been drinking. I asked if he had driven here drunk, and he replied that he was 'perfectly safe on the road.' I yelled at him for drunk driving but then got my cool back. I made him sit down on the couch and gave him a glass of water. He came to me for help. I was going to talk him through this.

He told me about how he felt out of control, how he blew all of the money he had left, and then he told me about a briefcase. He was slurring his words a bit, but apparently, he and a few friends stole it from someone and discovered the briefcase had some weird mystical power. According to drunk Jacob, who I didn't trust at all, the briefcase contained whatever the person reaching inside it desired most.

For Jacob, he said it was bottles upon bottles of tequila. I didn't believe what he said about the case, but he brought it with him, so I tested his theory and reached inside. There was a framed picture of my father and me on my tenth birthday. It wasn't real, though. He looked happy. In my memories, I knew for a fact my father wasn't happy that day.

Then I reached into the case again and I pulled out my ex-girlfriend's glasses. They still had the camera in them. They were stained with something. Tears? Maybe. I washed them off, and I understood. Jacob was telling the truth.

I was selfish. My greatest desire wasn't to help all of humanity, but rather to have a good relationship with my father and have my girlfriend feel bad about leaving me. I was not a good person.

Jacob asked if he could leave the briefcase with me. I let him stay the night in the spare bedroom and kept watch over the case. He was sober in the morning, so after a long talk where he swore to me he would never drive drunk again, I let him head home.

I kept the briefcase in my lab. I wanted to study it. I knew Jacob described it as some magical reality-altering thing, but I didn't believe in magic. I believed in science.

After all that happened, it almost felt like I was getting an irrational fear of answering the phone. Perhaps it wasn't irrational, though, as only a week into my studies with the case, I got another call from the man attempting to buy my research.

"Hello?"

"Bring the briefcase to Jacob's apartment in the next three hours, or I'll leave his decapitated head in a box on your porch."

The man on the other end of the line hung up.

My first reaction was panic.

I was terrified, but I knew I only had one choice.

I got in my car and drove to Jacob's home.

The entire ride there was full of thoughts about who this man was and why he would hurt Jacob, but I couldn't build a solid hypothesis.

My glasses fogged when I walked through Jacob's door, which was left unlocked. Jacob lived in a mansion. The place felt empty, almost dead in a sense. I could hear the echo of each step I took.

"I have the briefcase! Let my friend go!" I shouted.

There was no response.

"Hello," I called out.

"Upstairs," I heard a stern voice shout.

I walked through the front foyer and discovered Jacob, tied down to an office chair with tape over his mouth, and a man in a suit with a gun pointed at Jacob's head.

"Put the briefcase down. I wouldn't want to get any blood on it," the man demanded.

I left the case on the bottom step of the staircase and backed away.

"Now leave," he said.

"What about Jacob," I said, "let him go first."

"I'm not letting Jacob go, and if you don't get out, I'll shoot you where you stand," he said.

"Who are you?" I asked, "and what do you want with him? He hasn't done anything! You need to let him go!"

"My name is Loch, and I am the most powerful man in your godforsaken universe. Now get the hell out," he said.

"I've got you there," I told him. "You may think you're smart with your whole plan here, but my glasses have a hidden camera that has been recording this entire conversation. If I don't make it back home safe with Jacob, that video will automatically be sent to the police department, the FBI, Channel Four News, and be uploaded straight onto YouTube."

"You can't defy me, Anatta. I am a God. I am a fucking God, Anatta! You should have taken my deal."

He fired his gun, and the bullet struck the centre of my head.

Someone was saying something.
I could hear it, but just barely.

Get out of my head. You're the only thing left in my way. If you don't leave, I'll find a way to kill you myself.

How else am I supposed to watch the show? I need this front-row seat. We had a fair exchange.

Is this all a game to you?

You seem to be having fun with it—lots of fun.

I'm getting the power I've always deserved. Soon enough, I'll be able to kill you."

The second voice let out a horrible, high-pitched laugh. Both voices faded out, and I began to remember what had happened.

P24102!

Anatta!

Wake up!

Wake up!

I can't make it out of here without you.

I can't make it out of here without you.

I need you.

I need you.

You can't leave me like this.

You can't.

You saved me. I can't let you die.

You saved me. I can't let you die.

Please, just wake up.

Please, just wake up.

Please, just wake up.

Anatta?

Identity

"Hey, wake up!" I called out.

I heard my voice echo.

"P24102! You're awake! You were out for a long time. We started to get worried," '03 said. Liquorice meowed in agreement.

"I'm okay, don't worry about me," I said with a slight headache.

The green shard burst with light, then faded back to black.

"Wait, what happened to the guy that found us?" I asked.

"I think he's gone," '03 replied.

I quickly hushed him, hearing the footsteps again.

"We need to sneak out," I said. "Now. Follow me."

'03 and Liquorice followed me as we crept along the wall, attempting to stay out of sight.

"Jacob. Stop. We just need to talk," the guard shouted at me.

I didn't believe him.

The green shard began to flash again, and the guard began to run towards us. I lifted the gem in my hand and turned away, preparing for my final moments of existence free of torture, and—

The

Shard

Shot

A

Beam

Of

Light

At

The

Guard

Leaving

Only

Dust.

The green gem lost its light.

"Did we just- kill him?" I asked.

"He should come back to life, right," '03 said. "That's what the simulation, sorry, the Orb, always does."

"But this thing is a shard from the Heart- I've never seen anything like it. How do we know we didn't do something... permanent?"

"We can't stick around to find out. Look, let's just see if he left anything we could use."

"You go ahead. I'll wait," I said, nervous.

Liquorice was hiding behind my leg. He must have been terrified.

"I found something," '03 shouted back towards us.

"Bring it here," I shouted back.

'03 lugged a heavy-looking briefcase over to Liquorice and me and dropped it in front of us. "Let's open it up!"

Did I kill someone?

I couldn't have killed someone.

I am a good person.

I do good things.

I am a good person.

I do good things.

I am a terrible, worthless piece of shit that should rot in hell for murdering someone who was trying to do their job.

No.

I might not have murdered him.

I am a good person.

I try to be a good person.

Why can't I be a good person?

I need to be a good person.

How do you do it, Liquorice?

You never killed anyone, and you seem to make everyone happy.

Could I be a cat in my next life, or did I already do that one?

No.

Wait.

What have I done?

I want to be a good person.

Please, God, or whoever is up there, let me be a good person.

I want to be a good person.

I want him to live.

I didn't mean to kill him.

I'm going to destroy this crystal the second I get a chance.

What if he's dead forever now?

I need to be a good person, please.

Please, God, someone, whoever, make me a good person.

"What's inside the case," I asked.

"I can't see inside of it, but the case has something written on the side," '03 said, staring at the case from different angles.

"What does it say?"

"'This case holds your greatest desire,'" he replied, squinting to read the text.

"Try reaching inside."

"You try. I'm not going first."

"Fine."

I reached inside, and felt a piece of paper. It was strange considering how heavy the case was.

"It's a piece of paper that says 'Jacob' on it."

"How is that your greatest desire?"

"Well, it's a name? That's something I've always wanted. Jacob, though? I don't know if it fits."

"Just agree to the bloody name and move on."

"Jacob. Maybe it will grow on me," I said.

"Can I try next?"

"Sure thing, '03."

'03 reached into the briefcase. It was empty. He let out a laugh.

"I get it. Good point case."

"What do you mean? You didn't get anything?"

"Don't worry about it. Let's make our way out of here."

"Liquorice hasn't gotten his turn yet," I said.

An Ode to Belphegor

At the bottom of the pit at the bottom of the Orb.

There is a painter.

His paint is blood.

He's low on canvas.

The walls have eyes.

He made murals.

He found beauty in the pit's endless brawls.

He fetches water

From the ponds.

He cleans blood

From the walls so he can paint them yet again.

And he never frets over the erasure of his old work.

It is impermanent.

As

Everything

Should

Be.

In an infinite cycle of "torture" that all others deem hell.
But to the painter that embraces the absurd cycle.
It is heaven.

I II III IV V VI VII VIII IX X XI XII. I
I II III IV V VI VII VIII IX X XI XII. II
I II III IV V VI VII VIII IX X XI XII. III

I II III
I II III IV V VI VII VIII IX X XI. V
I II III

"Jacob, P24102, whatever your name is, I think the static is getting worse. We need to hurry," '03 said.

Liquorice pulled a ball of yarn from the briefcase.

"Alright, let's go. We can leave the briefcase behind," I replied. "I just have one thing left to do. I need to get rid of something."

I put the green shard in the briefcase so we could leave it there forever. As soon as I did that, though, the dust on the ground started shaking.

"Well, Jacob, good news, you didn't permanently kill anyone."

"Oh no."

'03, Liquorice, and I ran back onto our way before the man searching for us returned to life. We kept on track for a few hours before taking a break.

"We're getting close to escaping," I said. "What do you think is going to happen once we're out there?"

"Heaven, maybe?"

"How do we know we aren't going to end up someplace even worse than the Orb, though?" I asked.

"I guess we don't know until we make it out."

We all stopped.

"Why are we trying to escape?"

"We're in prison. That's what you do in prisons. You escape because you don't like being there."

"We had eternal life here," I said. "What if we're giving that up for good? Or, what if there's nothing out there? What if we just get forced to start over?"

"You sound like me."

"But for real. Here, we have food brought to us every day. We get to live a different life whenever we want. Could this be heaven?"

"Jacob, you could stay in the Orb. Stay in a prison cell for eternity. Sure, you'd be happy sometimes, but do you remember what we looked like when we thought escape was hopeless. Back when we thought living in the Orb was our only choice. You were picking fights with guards, and I was bashing my head against a wall. If you want to keep living like that, stay behind, but if not, come with me."

"03," I said, "if I don't see you on the other side, I'm going to miss you."

"I'm going to miss you too, Jacob."

Liquorice meowed.

The three continued to journey onwards. At the edge of the world, there was an abyss of static. They walked in.

I Need to Be a Good Person

P24102 jolted awake. He had escaped the Orb. Something was wrong, though. A woman was bleeding out at the bottom of the staircase. P24102, meanwhile, was tied to an office chair with tape over his mouth, and his memories were slowly coming back to him.

Jacob tried to scream through the tape Loch had put over his mouth.

"Did you finally make it out of the Orb?" Loch asked as he slowly ripped the tape off.

"Why would you do that? She did exactly what you told her to do! Why did you hurt her?" Jacob shouted.

"You did make it out, didn't you? I just wanted to see the look on your face," Loch said, laughing.

"You're dead. Channel Four and the FBI— she told you— they're going to know what you did. Everyone is going to know what you did," Jacob said.

"I own Channel Four, Jacob. I own the police force, and I own the FBI. I just thought this would be hilarious. Telling you your entire spiritual, magical journey was just me fucking with you," Loch said.

"What?" Jacob asked.

At the bottom of the staircase, a pool of blood was forming around Anatta's body. The blood was painting the white rug red. A cat with white, fluffy fur emerged from a hidden corner and was inspecting the scene.

"Oh God, you are behind. Jacob, please tell me, what does the briefcase do?" Loch asked.

"It gives you your greatest desire, right?" Jacob asked with tears in his eyes.

"Exactly," Loch said. "You should've noticed something was wrong when you pulled out a bottle of tequila."

"What was wrong?" Jacob asked, his face turning red.

The cat at the bottom of the staircase took a few paces around Annata's corpse, careful not to let the blood stain its fur.

"Your greatest desire was to be a good person, Jacob," Loch said. "Apparently, the only way to do that was by teaching you a lesson in a weird sci-fi prison. The briefcase created the Orb."

"The second I'm out of here, I'm going to kill you," Jacob said.

Behind Loch was a painting with a golden frame. It was massive in scale. The painting depicted a man standing on a dirt road. On the man's left was a casual-looking gas station, and on his right was a staircase leading into the heavens.

"Sure, you will," Loch said dismissively. "Listen, the Orb was supposed to be a spiritual journey for you Jacob. You started by living through a terrible version of your own life. A world where you made all the wrong choices. Then, you were supposed to live through the lives of moral philosophers, activists, and a bunch of other morally righteous fools. They were supposed to teach you something before being reborn into your old life."

"What went wrong then?" Jacob asked, trying to break his hands out of the binds. "What did you do?"

"You know, it could have been a beautiful story," Loch said, "a feel-good movie maybe. Fun for the whole family. Instead, I went and found your address. I needed to take back what was mine. My briefcase. The one you and your friends, Abraham and Isaac, decided to steal."

"What?" Jacob asked.

"Jacob, I found the Orb. It's designed pretty similarly to the computers we have in the outside world. I have a whole research team that helps me with this sort of thing. We quickly discovered we could both control the Jacob inside of the Orb, and the Jacob outside of the Orb."

"What do you mean?" Jacob asked.

"The Orb let me take control of you, use your life as bait to lure your friend here, and it let me kill her in front of you."

"You are insane," Jacob said.

"No, Jacob, I am God," Loch said, "and I destroy those who defy me. I found some real pitiful lives for you to live through. We ran the one where you died alone in space at least a dozen times. It was beautiful."

As Loch raised his voice, the white cat ran off in fear. Anatta's body continued to rest atop the rug, undisturbed.

"Are the people in there- the people- are they real?" Jacob stuttered.

"I took anyone who pissed me off and threw them in the Orb. I started with that annoying cat. He was our test subject. Then anytime someone said no to me, even after I offered them money, I would just throw them into the Orb, have my team take control of their mind once they were in there, and force them to say yes instead," Loch said.

"You can't do that. I won't let this happen. I don't care if you ruined my life or made me die repeatedly. All I care about is the fact that you killed my completely innocent friend."

"I could've thrown her into the Orb, but I thought this would be more entertaining. Look at you, crying. This is the highlight of my day. I should have brought a camera."

"What happens now, Loch? I already escaped. Are you just going to kill me?" Jacob asked.

"No, Jacob, of course not. That wouldn't be as fun."

Loch pulled a black Orb out of his pocket. A light shone out of it and onto Jacob.

"This will just take a second," Loch said.

In a mere moment, all of Jacob's work to escape was rendered useless. He returned to the Orb.

Acknowledgements

Thank you to my wonderful parents and supportive friends. I'd also like to thank my friends Dana and Jasmine for designing the cover!

About the Author

Colin Dunbar is a young Canadian author. He is a university student currently studying English as well as Criminal Justice and Public Policy. He is also the author of a collection of short stories called *Sanity in the Absurd*.

Also by Colin Dunbar:

Sanity in the Absurd

Sanity in the Absurd is a collection of ten interconnected short stories by Colin Dunbar. One story follows a man who discovers a store where he can buy and sell time. Another story is about a woman attempting to climb the world's tallest building and fighting against self-doubt. A third story is about a person that finds a strange USB sewn into a backpack, then uses an online forum to attempt to discover the secrets it holds.

If you want to read ten complex, creative stories that are complemented by unique uses of colour, *Sanity in the Absurd* is the book for you!

Recommended for ages 16+

Note: Due to the format of the stories, the e-book version has an alternate ending.

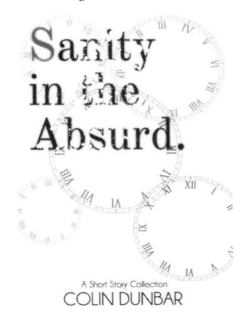

Coming Soon

The Era of the Orb: Volume Two

For updates:

Visit my Website: readcolin.com or readcolin.ca

Follow me on Instagram: @colinbdunbar

Manufactured by Amazon.ca
Bolton, ON